Christmas at Cedar Creek

Pine Harbor Series
Allison's Pine Harbor Summer
Evelyn's Pine Harbor Autumn
Lydia's Pine Harbor Christmas

Holiday House Novels
The Christmas Cabin
The Winter Lodge
The Lighthouse
The Christmas Castle
The Beach House
The Christmas Tree Inn
The Holiday Hideaway

Highland Passage Series
Highland Passage
Knight Errant
Lost Bride

Highland Soldiers Series
The Enemy

The Betrayal
The Return
The Wanderer

Highland Vow

American Hearts Romances
Secret Hearts
Runaway Hearts
Forbidden Hearts

For more information, visit jljarvis.com.

THE LIGHTHOUSE

THE LIGHTHOUSE

A HOLIDAY HOUSE NOVEL

J.L. JARVIS

THE LIGHTHOUSE
A Holiday House Novel

Published by Bookbinder Press
bookbinderpress.com

ISBN 978-1-942767-26-8 (trade paperback)
ISBN 978-1-942767-08-4 (paperback)
ISBN 978-1-942767-07-7 (ebook)

ONE

EMILY COOKE SET the last box of books on the floor by her suitcase and went straight to the back porch that faced the sea. There was no one about, which was just fine with her. To the left, within walking distance, stood an old lighthouse that embodied everything that she'd wanted for her yearlong escape from the life she had known. The old lightkeeper's house stood at the edge, where the land met the water that stretched to the horizon—where the sky, in turn, went on forever. The sight of it lifted the weight of the past several years from her shoulders. She drew in a deep breath of salt air and sighed as the gentle breeze rustled the grass on the dunes. She had rented this place for a year in order to lose herself in something so vast and timeless that her life would seem small and safe in its presence.

She'd longed for that feeling at the end of each

class and every evening in the months since her mother had died. Almost two years before, her ailing aunt had moved in with Emily and her mother when she'd grown too ill to care for herself. She was gone six months later. Right after that, her mother's health had declined from the same hereditary disease and in almost the same way as her aunt's. And now they were gone. Emily was alone.

She reclined, rested her head on the back of the chair, and felt nothing but bliss. She took in the rush and retreat of the foam-laced seawater on sand and the cries of the gulls as they circled the lighthouse nearby.

And a loud rumbling motor.

Emily got up and went to the side of the back porch to see what it could be. With her hands on the rail, she leaned over and looked toward the front of her small rental cottage. Next door, a man pulled into the driveway astride an old motorcycle. He parked the old red rumbly thing and pulled off his helmet. A mass of straight espresso-brown hair fell to his shoulders. He turned just enough for her to catch a glimpse of his face, which had too much growth to be stubble yet not quite enough to be a beard. *Oh, great. I've moved in next door to Grizzly McStubble and his thundering motorcycle. So much for my quiet haven.*

He cast a sidelong glance at her. Since she was already leaning halfway over the rail for no plausible reason except to look at him, she couldn't pretend she didn't see him. And they were going to be neighbors, so what else could she do but ignore her annoyance and wave? She almost managed a smile. He was looking right at her, but he turned without so much as a wave or hello and walked into his garage.

Emily stared in disbelief. "Well, okay, then." She shrugged and returned to her chair. So her new neighbor was rude. Or maybe he thought she was interested in him and didn't want to get her hopes up. She smiled wryly. He could let go of that notion. She had no feelings left but the gentle numbness of being alone. And since everything else in Hope Harbor was perfect, she would have to adjust to his antisocial proclivity. In fact, the more she thought about it, the more she believed it was better that way. Having a tacit agreement to ignore one another worked right into her plan for her one year of solitude.

EMILY SAT up abruptly then looked about for a moment before she remembered where she was. The faint glow of late afternoon hung in the air. She had dozed off in the porch chair, in the afternoon, no less—something she rarely did. But she'd come to the beach house to relax and, at some point, to finish her dissertation.

She glanced at her watch. She didn't know how late stores stayed open, so she decided to make a quick run for some groceries. After combing her fingers through her plain brown shoulder-length hair, she arranged it in a knot at the nape of her neck, grabbed her car keys, and headed out the door.

Grizzly McStubble was back outside working on that old beat-up motorcycle of his. She couldn't help but notice the impressive array of tools strewn about him. Emily headed for her car, poised to wave just in case he looked up. He did not. Well, at least she'd been willing to give him the benefit of the doubt. She got into her car and backed out of the driveway. Her seat-belt alarm went off, so she pulled the belt over and locked it. The alarm kept going, and so did she. After she'd made a right turn onto the road, her car sputtered and stopped directly in front of Grizzly McStubble's cottage.

She turned the key again. Nothing. "Crap." She exhaled, exasperated. In her *everything's going to be fine* voice, she said "Okay" a handful of times as if repeating it might make it so. She dug through her purse, pulled out her phone, and began scrolling through search results for a service station nearby.

A tapping at the driver's-side window made her

flinch. She turned to find Grizzly McStubble staring at her with a quizzical look, a well-worn T-shirt clinging to his muscular shoulders and chest. Not that she was interested, but how could she not notice? She was merely observing the obvious. In spite of her recent stint at nonelective celibacy, she still recognized an attractive man when she saw one.

Emily pressed the button to open her window. Nothing happened. She looked up at him. He was talking—she could hear his voice but not what he was saying. He made a key-turning motion with his hand, which confused her for a moment. He pointed at the ignition. *Of course.* The window couldn't open without power. She knew that. She turned the key, pressed the button, and the window came down. *Brilliant, Em. Stunningly brilliant.* This was yet one more reason why she had chosen to retreat from the world. She didn't like feeling awkward, which was an all-too-familiar state of mind for her around men—although, to be honest, college-faculty types weren't always the smoothest, at least not in her department. Grace and poise took practice, and she didn't have the best talent pool to draw from.

He studied her with a quizzical frown. "Something wrong?"

"Uh, no. I was just thinking. I frown when I think." *About eyes.* His were not bad, she had to admit—deep set, the kind a girl could get lost in. But she knew what came next. The men she interacted with had come down to three types: helpers, fixers, and sleepers—none of which interested her at the moment.

"I mean with your car." His eyes shone with amusement, probably at her expense.

"Oh. I don't know. I've been driving all day. It's been fine. But just now, I don't know. It just quit. It won't start."

He nodded as though deep in thought.

Emily waited, expecting him to speak. When he didn't, she said, "Well, anyway, I'll call someone and have the car out of your way soon."

He shook his head as he frowned and stared into the distance.

Since he wasn't sharing any of those deep, silent thoughts, she exhaled. "Well, thank you. I'll just make a few calls. I'll be fine. I'm sure you have more important things to do." *Like buy a new T-shirt since your muscles might stretch that one out of shape.*

As she picked up her phone, she made a mental note that she really had to make an effort to be more observant, since she'd clearly misjudged him—his looks anyway. She could only see from the waist up. It was probably better that way, but so far, so good. If a little motorcycle noise could so easily distract her from the beauty that existed in nature—and neighbors—it was no wonder she was still single. *Sort of single.*

"Get out of the car."

"Excuse me?" she said.

"Let me take a look."

So he was a fixer—and a bossy one at that. But her car needed fixing, and he had all of those tools. With a shrug, she got out of the car.

He was grinning but at her expense—she was certain of it.

She sidled past him as they switched places. "I might have missed an oil change or two."

"Don't do that," he said.

"Uh, okay. Good to know, but too late."

He started to get in but turned back to face her—clearly as an afterthought, but better late than never. He extended his hand. "Wes Taggert." He looked into her eyes.

There were defining moments in life. In that moment, she gained a complete understanding of how blue eyes could be—and how shallow she was. She had never known a gaze so intense as to weaken one's knees. And as much as she would have enjoyed a good swoon in his arms right then, the timing was wrong.

From somewhere deep inside, a reflex took over, and she managed to reach for his outstretched hand and shake it. "Emily Cooke." She quickly averted her eyes lest his gaze send her IQ further south than it already was.

"Excuse me." He gestured toward the front seat, which she was blocking.

"Oh, sorry." She stepped out of the way, and he got into the car.

When he turned the key, nothing happened. He turned it again, then he stared at the dashboard. Moments later, he got out of the car. "Did you hear anything when you were driving?"

"My music."

"Loud music?"

"Maybe." She winced.

"Did you see any lights on the dashboard?"

Emily frowned and thought for a moment. "Not really."

He studied her as if she'd just lost her mind. "You're out of gas."

"Oh, that. But whenever it goes off, I always have plenty of time to get to a station."

"Not this time. You're past empty, and the fuel-gauge warning light's on."

She thought she detected a smirk, although he seemed to be making an effort to suppress it. She started to nod as though deep in thought, which she wasn't. She was stuck. After three years of tending to her mother and aunt and taking care of their health-care, insurance, and everything else—after seeing them laid to rest—here she was. She had held on and powered through. But now, she'd arrived at the refuge she'd dreamed of, and she'd let down her guard. And she couldn't start her car. She knew what to do, but she couldn't seem to take one step to do it.

He ran his fingers through his hair. "On the plus side, you've got amazing powers of concentration." He grinned.

Emily couldn't help but offer a nervous smile back, which brought her to her senses. "Well, thank you for your help." She turned to go into her cottage and make a few phone calls. There had to be a service station nearby. She felt the phone in her hand and hoped he wouldn't notice. The truth was, she just wanted to go. Meltdowns were better in private.

"What're you doing?"

"Going to call someone." She slipped her phone into her back pocket.

He shook his head. "I'll take you into town for some gas."

"Oh, I couldn't."

"It's no trouble."

She eyed the motorcycle. "I'm not going anywhere on that."

His assessing look made her feel as though she'd just lost his respect. "We'll take my car." He took a step toward the garage and said over his shoulder, "Come on."

"Sorry. It's nothing personal. I just have a policy of not getting into cars with strangers."

He looked a bit stunned for a second but recovered. "You're right." He nodded, more to himself than to her, then he turned and walked away.

Emily called after him, "But thanks anyway." Without turning, he waved and walked into his house. She'd offended him—that much was clear. But she'd rather offend him than get into the car of a man she'd just met, even if he was good-looking. Especially if he was good-looking. Chances were, he was a nice guy trying to do a nice thing. A nice guy would understand that—or be offended, as he apparently was. But she owed him no apology for being smart and protecting herself.

In any event, he was gone, and she needed a tow truck. She gave up on going inside and sank into the car seat to search her phone for a service station. Wes backed a black status car out of the garage and drove off. He'd bailed. That resolved any question of whether he was offended. She wasn't happy about it, but she couldn't think of what she could have done differently. So she turned her attention to the matter at hand, found a station on the Internet, and called for a tow truck.

Twenty minutes later, Emily was sitting in the driver's seat, waiting and checking her email, when Wes pulled back into his driveway. Emily watched him over the top of her phone and debated whether to approach him and apologize for her lack of tact. They were going to be neighbors, and an apology might smooth over any awkwardness between them. She got out of the car, but before she could speak, he opened his trunk and pulled out a gas can. She wasn't expecting that after the way he had left.

"Pop the door to your gas tank."

"Okay." So he hadn't been offended after all. He was simply a man of few words, which threw her a little off balance. As she watched him empty the gas can into her tank, a tow truck pulled up. Emily walked over to the driver. "I'm so sorry. My neighbor has helped me out, so I won't be needing your services after all."

He glanced over at Wes then shook his head. "Sorry, lady, but you're still gonna have to pay for the call since I made the trip out here."

She nodded and handed him her credit card. "I understand."

He shrugged. "If I made free business trips to everyone who called, my kids would go hungry."

Emily smiled at him. "That's okay. I understand completely. No problem."

He looked a little confused to miss out on an argument he'd so clearly expected. Then he shrugged and handed her credit card back to her. "Well, okay, then."

Emily signed for the charge, and he went on his way. She returned to find Wes emerging from his garage. She opened her mouth to thank him, but he held out his hand. "Keys?"

She put them in his outstretched palm. He got into the car and turned the key. Nothing happened. He gave it two more tries, and it started. From the look on Wes's face as he watched her face light up, she realized she might have overreacted. But having a functioning car meant she had regained control of her life.

He smiled, and she couldn't help but smile back. "I don't know how to thank you. I didn't expect you to do that."

He shrugged. "We're neighbors."

"Well, I know, but—well, thank you." She felt as though she should shake his hand, but she just thanked him again and turned to go to her car. "Oh, wait! You paid for the gas. Here, just a minute." She reached into her purse, pulled out her wallet, and took in a sharp breath. "Oh." She looked up at him and winced. "I'm so sorry. I don't have any cash."

He smiled. "Don't worry about it."

She shook her head. "But I will. I promise I'll pay

you back when I get back from the store. How much was it?"

His face wrinkled into a smirk, as if he thought she was being ridiculous. "Consider it a housewarming gift."

"But I don't even know you."

He gave her a curious look. "You know, most people would just take the money and run."

"I'm not most people." There was more truth to that than she cared to admit.

"I'm beginning to realize that." The corner of his mouth turned up to hint at a smile. He lowered his chin and looked up at her. "You'd better get going before the store closes."

Emily was still frowning when he turned and walked away. There was no sense in arguing the point. She would just have to pay him back later.

Without turning, he called back to her, "Fill up that tank when you get into town."

"Okay." She got into her car. As she fastened her seatbelt, she stole a glance at Wes, who was sitting on an old tire, back at work on his bike.

TWO

EMILY PUT away the last of her groceries except for a six-pack of local craft beer. She put a twenty for the gas into a thank-you card and slipped the envelope between a bottle and the cardboard carton. It was nearly dark outside, but she could still see enough to make her way to her neighbor's front door.

"I'm back here," he called out from his back deck.

That wasn't part of the plan. She'd expected to leave the six-pack on his front porch in stealth mode then return to her cottage with no actual contact. Instead, she rounded the corner to find him on his deck, comfortably ensconced in a chair with his feet propped up on another chair. She reached over the rail and offered the six-pack. "I wanted to thank you again."

As he took it, the thank-you card fell to the ground. He reached down and started to return it to her.

"No, that's for you. For the gas."

He frowned his disapproval at her.

She met his gaze frankly. "I don't like owing money."

He shook his head. "Emily Cooke." Then he glanced at the beer, pulled out two bottles, and held one out to her.

"Oh. No thanks."

He shrugged and put back the bottle.

"I've got unpacking to do," she said just to fill the silence.

With a glint in his eye, he gave a slight nod then leaned his head back against the deck chair. She couldn't help but think he saw through her excuse, but he didn't call her on it. In fact, he didn't say a word.

Emily glanced toward her cottage. "Well, good night, then."

He glanced toward her. "Good night, Emily Cooke."

She walked back to her cottage, went straight to her own six-pack of beer in the fridge, and pulled out a chilled bottle. She held it to her temple for a moment then twisted the cap off and took a drink. Wes Taggert made her uneasy. Once she'd gotten a good look up close, it became clear that behind her new neighbor's unkempt hair and overgrown whiskers was a man with piercing eyes and an understated confidence that rendered her constantly struggling to maintain her balance. In other words, he was trouble.

Emily shook her head. This was not going to happen. She had no room in her life at the moment for that kind of chemistry.

WES TAGGERT SAT on his deck, looking into the shadows. It was too dark to see out to sea, but the sound and the smell of saltwater and grass soothed his senses. The beer in his hand didn't hurt, either. *Thank you, Emily Cooke.* He held up his beer in a toast and contemplated the events that had led him to a point where his life lay in ruins. Beer was the only thing he could thank her for. He'd come to the seaside to escape. And yet here she was—another woman to become entangled in his life. *Dude, you've gone over the edge now. She isn't the sort to do that.* But even with those glasses and all of that hair pulled back into a bun, he could see that she really was the sort.

He shut his eyes. She was so wrong for him. She was the kind of woman who gave all of her heart, body, and soul—the sort who would break just from being with him. He couldn't do that to her.

He reminded himself of why he'd come to the beach—to get away from all the duplicitous excrement he'd once embraced when he'd arrived at his career goal. He'd enjoyed that life—at least until he got to the part where it all hit the fan, and it didn't go well after that. One day and one act had cost him six months in jail. When he got out, he moved into this cottage, where he spent the next five months drinking beer, working on his 1946 motorcycle, and staring out at the sea.

And now Wes Taggert was lonely. Not for sex. He could get that when he wanted it—most of the time anyway. But sex wasn't the same thing as looking at someone and knowing whatever you did on that day would be better with her. He missed that. Well, correction—he'd never known that, not really. But he wanted it. He blamed his new need on the sea and the sound of the wind in the tall bending grass on the dunes. They made a man contemplate his life.

He'd had too much to drink. When he was starting to think of the meaning of life, it was time to go inside and let go of the day.

EMILY WENT FOR A WALK. It was dawn, and she'd woken two hours before. She had thought she might get past the insomnia that continually plagued her, but no such luck. So she'd had two cups of coffee and waited until the sun rose. It was well worth the wait. Alone on the beach, she could go where she wanted. There was no need to think or solve problems.

Except for the car. There'd been a moment when she'd feared she would lose control and spill her emotions all over her neighbor's driveway, and all because her car had run out of gas. Of all the problems she'd dealt with over the past few years, why would her car be the one to derail her? She knew the answer already: no one depended on her anymore to be strong, so she wasn't. She could only be grateful she'd managed to conceal her lack of strength from Wes.

Wes Taggert. How had he gotten inside her head? What she needed was a run—a good, long, vigorous run. So she ran along the wet, packed sand of the shore-line. If she'd known how good this would feel, she'd have longed for it sooner—but not as much as she longed for her mother and aunt.

A pang of guilt seized her. Whenever she almost forgot to be sad, something would remind her of the loved ones she'd lost, and remorse would seize her. Her therapist had told her she needed to give herself permission to be happy again. She knew it was okay to be happy, but she would remember her mother and aunt when they were young and energetic, and the image would fade to one of rented hospital beds and equipment. It was part of the circle of life, but the circle of life was too cruel.

Emily stopped, gasping for air. She looked up at the lighthouse before her. At one time, it had shone out to sea, guiding ships safely to shore. She had always loved lighthouses, even though she'd grown up away from the water. There was something so timeless and comforting about them—their stalwart presence and purpose of leading the lost homeward. In fact, she had chosen to rent her cottage because of its view of the lighthouse. Of the many important decisions she'd made over the past couple of years, this one might have been her best. She felt as if she'd come home—but it was a home without sorrow.

Her run to the lighthouse had come at a cost. She had pushed herself too hard and had to make the return trip walking and wobbly kneed. She started to wonder when she'd gotten so out of shape, but she knew the answer—when her care for others' health had to come before hers.

As she drew close to home, she sensed she was not alone. She hadn't noticed any movement, yet something drew her to furtively glance toward the neighboring cottage. She wanted to blame it on some sort of mystical second sight, but the truth was that she looked because she couldn't help herself. And there he was, in the mottled shadows of his covered deck, with his coffee. Their eyes met, but she averted her gaze so quickly that he couldn't have known she had seen him. At least, that was her hope.

As she walked inside through the back door, she heard a knock at the front door. Her heart skipped a beat as she wondered if it could be Wes. Preparing herself, she slowly pulled open the door. "Mrs. Langdon. Hello." There stood her landlady, a woman slightly shorter than Emily's five feet six inches. She had a shock of cropped steel-gray hair contained by a wide-brimmed straw hat. She wore her usual uniform of loose-fitting short-sleeved shirt and shorts and thickly treaded hiking sandals.

"Please call me Delia."

"Delia," Emily echoed with a smile. "Come in."

"Oh, I don't want to interrupt."

"You're not interrupting at all. I just got back from a run, and I was about to make some coffee. Why don't you join me?"

Delia's eyes twinkled when she smiled. "Well, okay. Just for a minute. Then I'll let you get on with your day."

She followed Emily into the kitchen, and they exchanged small talk while Emily made the coffee. She handed Delia a cup. "It's such a nice day. Would you mind if we went out on the porch?"

"No, that sounds lovely."

As they settled into the chairs on her back porch, Emily noticed that Wes had gone inside. She ignored the tiny pang of disappointment she had no business feeling.

Delia got to the point and handed Emily a brochure she'd pulled from her pocket. "I know you just moved in, but I'm canvassing the neighborhood to let people know about a cause that's important to me and to many who live here."

Emily nodded with genuine interest. She had no pet cause—she just wanted to get involved in the community in order to draw her attention to anything but her own life. She skimmed the brochure. "Oh, the lighthouse! I love it. You know, that's one of the reasons I rented this cottage. I love that view."

Delia nodded. "We all do. The lighthouse is part of our landscape and part of our history. But it's old and in need of repair. Things have gotten so bad that there's talk of just tearing it down. No one really wants that, but there isn't enough money to do the work needed to keep it standing."

A sinking feeling caught Emily off guard. Why did she care this deeply? She'd barely unpacked. Still, it mattered to her.

Delia continued. "We are looking for donations."

Emily stood. "I'll go get my checkbook."

"Actually, we've got a website that's handling donations. The information is on the brochure. If you go to this link, you can donate with just a few clicks." She leaned forward as if telling a secret. "I think it's their way of making sure I don't take the money and run."

Emily laughed. "I'm sure that's just what they were thinking when they set up the website. You look like the nefarious type."

"You'd be surprised—not about me, mind you, but real-life criminals don't look at all like they do in the cop shows. They just look like regular people." A faraway look came and went. Delia turned back to Emily and smiled. "Anyway, whatever you can give would be great."

"I'm happy to give what money I can. What I have even more of is time. I'd be happy to help if there's anything you think I could do." She felt a bit strange making a decision on impulse. For so long, her life had been ruled by good sense and planning. But already, she loved that old lighthouse. Moreover, she needed a project, and this one fit the bill.

"It's short notice, but if you're not busy, there's a meeting tomorrow at the community center."

Emily hesitated. The meeting was sooner than she'd expected, but she didn't really have any plans. "Well, I don't see why not."

Delia's face brightened. "Good. Then I'll see you

tomorrow." She stood. "I won't keep you. And I have houses to visit. Oh! I'm so sorry. I didn't even ask, but it looks like you've settled in nicely."

Emily glanced about. "I've still got a little unpacking to do, but I love this place. I look forward to spending a year here."

As they went out to the front porch, Delia looked over next door. "And have you met your neighbor?"

"Yes, I have."

Delia lowered her voice conspiratorially. "There's something about him you might not notice at first: underneath all those handsome good looks is a very nice man." She studied Emily. "Are you single?"

Emily felt herself blush. She hadn't been prepared for Delia's directness. "I'm not in the market for male companionship."

Delia nodded with complete understanding. "Of course. How presumptuous of me. There's an LGBT group that meets once a week at the community center. I'm sure they'd welcome a new member. I could introduce you around."

Emily's eyes widened then relaxed as she smiled and explained, "No, I'm straight. I'm just not looking for romance."

Delia nodded as though it made perfect sense, although Emily barely understood it herself. The past couple of years had left her drained and wanting nothing more than solitude. But Delia had such a kind-ness about her that Emily found herself wanting to confide, although she held back because that was what she always did. Delia didn't push. She smiled sweetly and went on her way down the road to the next house.

Inside, Emily started unpacking one of the boxes of desk and research supplies. She pulled out her apple-shaped stress reliever and set it in its usual place beside her computer. The emotion caught in her throat. Her mother had gotten that for her when she'd started her college teaching job. Through the last several years, it had been there to remind her of her mother's faith in her.

Emily took in a deep breath and let it out slowly. Once she set up her work area, she'd be back in her element. In the toughest of times, her desk was where she came at the end of the day to pull herself back together. Over the next several months, she would finish the job. Until then, she had nothing to give—especially not to a relationship.

THREE

EMILY SAT AT THE TABLE, which now served as her desk, with only the table lamp and her computer monitor to light her corner of the room. A car pulled in next door. Anyone would have looked, but maybe not with so much interest. *Still, there's no harm in looking, right?* The car door opened and lit the driver's side enough for her to see someone get out and lift up a package. *Pizza delivery.* She rolled her eyes. *Okay, girl detective, maybe now you can solve the mystery of the empty fridge.* That pizza looked good. She wondered whether Wes was a straightforward pepperoni-pie man or preferred something more exotic like Hawaiian pizza.

She realized she'd been so caught up in her work that she hadn't eaten since lunch. She glanced at her watch. *My last meal was hours ago.* Though tempted,

Emily refrained from chasing after the pizza guy before he got into his car. Instead, she went into the kitchen and pulled out a frozen entrée to pop into the microwave. Then she returned to her desk. She would work until she got to a stopping point then call it a night.

W ES COULDN'T SLEEP. In that respect, it was a normal night. He barely thought anymore of his life in the city during the day, but more nights than not, he woke up wondering how he could have avoided his unfortunate fate. With no resolution to that nagging question, he would usually get up and sit out on the back deck, listening to the sea, until weariness won out over nagging regret.

But that night, when he went out and sat down, a light drew his attention. Behind the thin linen curtain, his neighbor was pacing. Then the hazy silhouette stopped and sank down. Judging from the unnatural glow, she was at her computer. Wes couldn't imagine a lonelier place than a computer at night. *Not like sitting alone in the dark on your deck, you jackass.* For him, a computer had been the portal to a vast landscape of people in cubicles doing work that they thought was important. But life had a way of putting things into perspective.

He sighed and looked away. All that mattered in life was what people hadn't managed to ruin, which to his way of thinking was the sky and the sea and the feel of the sand underfoot. Those were the things that brought him back to his senses after he'd left all the madness of work.

Emily's light went out. *Well, at least someone is going to get some sleep tonight.*

THE COMMUNITY CENTER was humming with conversation and activity. Everyone seemed to know everyone else—except Emily. But this was the sort of place she wanted to be, and the lighthouse was the sort of cause she could believe in. The lighthouse preservation meeting was held in a large central room. It looked as though there were dozens of people. Seeing the turnout renewed her faith in humanity, or at least in her new community. She was glad she'd arrived early and claimed a seat by draping her sweater over a chair. She went to a long table next to the wall and helped herself to a cup of coffee before she headed back to her seat. As the people began to find places to sit, the room grew quiet.

Emily was halfway to her seat when Wes Taggert made a last-minute entrance and sat down next to her sweater. For a brief moment, she considered giving it up. She had other sweaters. Did she really need this one? There were two problems with that. The first was that the only seats left were in the middle of rows, and she would have drawn notice climbing over knees to get to them. The second was that her sweater was part of a set, and she was wearing the sleeveless piece that matched it. So she braced herself and sat down.

Wes leaned closer. "I see Delia got to you too."

Emily turned and smiled politely. "I rented my cottage because of the lighthouse. I liked the view. I know it sounds silly, but it already means something to me. So when Delia told me about this, it seemed like a good cause. And I've got some spare time."

"Makes sense." He gave her a warm yet powerful smile that she felt down to her soul.

Though she was trying so hard not to risk getting involved, Emily found herself lighting up as she smiled right back. "What about you?"

"Me?"

"Why are you here? Did Delia strong-arm you?"

He looked a bit bashful. "Delia doesn't have to strong-arm me. She knows I'd do anything for her. If she wanted to, she could really take advantage of me."

Emily smirked. "Oh, too nice, are you?"

Wes leveled a look at her. "No, I've just known her since I was a boy. She got me started in business."

"Really?" Emily leaned back and studied him. For some reason, she hadn't thought of him as the entrepreneurial kind. She'd assumed he was just another of the trust-fund babies so commonly found in these parts.

With a glint in his eyes, Wes nodded. "She was my first lawn-mowing customer."

Emily's eyes narrowed, then a smile bloomed on her face.

"What?" He straightened his posture defensively.

"I was just trying to imagine you as a ten-year-old boy mowing lawns."

"Twelve. I started late building my empire."

"And what empire is that, if you don't mind my asking?"

A look of reserve clouded his eyes. "These days, my empire consists of the sand and the sea."

Unemployed, are you? Emily managed not to say it out loud, then the meeting began and removed the temptation.

As much as the lighthouse meant a lot to her, Emily found her mind wandering to the man beside her. She was acutely aware of his presence. But who wouldn't be? The word *attractive* didn't quite do him justice. There was something more. His hair was pulled back into a short ponytail, and his day-old stubble went well with his strong jaw line and full lips. He was dressed in a cleaner version of the only clothes she'd seen him in—a T-shirt and jeans. She found herself trying to decide whether he had a faint scent of cologne or herbal soap. Whatever it was, she wanted some for herself just to smell now and then—preferably with the man included. She looked down at his thigh, only inches from hers. *Whoa, Emily. You really need to get out more.* Lest she start drooling, she turned her attention to the speaker, who explained that a website had been set up where people could sign up for committees and donate their talent and money to the lighthouse.

Less than an hour later, the meeting ended. Emily picked up her empty coffee cup.

"Here, I'll take that." By the time Wes finished saying it, he'd already slipped his cup inside hers and taken the two cups in hand. He nodded in the direction of a trash can nearby. While the two of them waited for people beside them to clear the way to the aisle, Wes lobbed the cups into the trash can.

Emily couldn't help but turn toward him, impressed.

He shrugged. "I played a little basketball in high school."

"From a lawn-mowing mogul to a basketball jock.

That's quite a career progression." She smiled, making an effort to look casual, which she couldn't ever manage to feel around him.

"And what about Emily Cooke? What's your career progression?"

Emily tilted her head toward the now-clear aisle behind him. "Ah, here we go."

When they got to the end of the row, Wes stepped aside and extended his arm, inviting Emily to go first, then he followed her through the door. "I'll see you to your car."

"Thanks, but you don't have to."

He shook his head as if it were nothing. "It's the right thing to do."

Something about what he'd said caught her off guard. If he'd sat next to anyone else, would he have walked that person out too? She had a feeling he might have, so she said nothing and kept walking.

"This is it." She stopped by the door, keys in hand.

"Yes, I remember."

"Oh, yeah. I forgot about that." Emily felt heat come to her cheeks and hoped it was too dark for him to see.

He just stared at her with a spark in his eyes.

Emily's car chirped as she unlocked it. "Well, assuming I haven't run out of gas, I'll be on my way. Thank you."

"Good night, Emily."

She got into her car, and Wes closed the door for her. She couldn't remember the last time someone had closed a door for her—not that she needed or expected it, but she kind of liked it. The guy had some manners, which meant he was just being polite, and she had to relax. He would have done the same for anyone else. With that settled, her mind wandered to thoughts of how manly he was. *Oh my gosh, Emily. Stop!* If she didn't get her car on the road, he'd be tapping on her window again, so she pulled out of the parking space and headed for home.

It didn't take long for her thoughts to find their way back to Wes. *This is not going to happen. I don't need a friend, and I certainly don't need a boyfriend. He probably doesn't even want that. He's just being nice. And I'm losing my mind.*

FOUR

EMILY PUT down the phone and leaned on her elbows to stare at the computer monitor. She had offered her graphic-design skills to the lighthouse campaign, and they had quickly accepted. On the phone, the head of the committee had told her she'd be working with someone with extensive experience in the field of advertising, which sounded great until she mentioned his name. Wes Taggert in advertising? That would have been her last guess. He didn't exactly fit the profile. Those types were usually sharp dressers and perfectly groomed, neither of which described Wes. Regardless of how he appeared, the main issue for Emily was the fact that she and Wes would be working together. She took in a breath and exhaled slowly. *Okay.* So they'd be working together. It wasn't as though she couldn't work and play well with others.

She'd been working with others for years. None of them had been wildly attractive, but other than that, it would be just the same. She'd be all work and no play, and they'd get the job done. Simple as that.

An hour later, she stared past her computer to the ocean beyond. She had nothing. Every time she thought of an interesting angle for the lighthouse campaign, she'd second-guess herself and rule it out. She leaned back in her chair, exasperated. A knock at the door saved her from her misery—until she opened the door.

There stood Wes in a worn T-shirt and jeans, his uncombed hair pulled back into a man bun. "So it looks like we're working together." He smiled as though he didn't mind it at all, which surprised her.

Emily nodded. "Yeah, I didn't know you were in advertising."

"Well, it's not something I like to broadcast." He took in her questioning look. "I got out of the business."

"Oh?"

He smirked dismissively. "Yeah." The look on his face told her he wasn't going to say any more about that. He leaned against the doorjamb and stared off into the distance. There was a whole story in his eyes that he wasn't disclosing. She found herself searching for it nonetheless. With no warning, he turned his unsettling gaze to her. The next thing she knew, she was asking him in. What made her think that would help the situation was anyone's guess.

He glanced at her computer and the photo of the Hope Harbor Lighthouse front and center. "Oh, I see you've already begun." He pulled over the closest chair and sat down beside her.

"Not exactly. I was just soaking it in, looking for inspiration."

He nodded approvingly. "So you're a graphic designer?"

"Yes."

"Where?"

"Oh, well, now I teach it at a junior college."

"Didn't like the business world?"

She knew they would get to that sooner or later. She'd left the business world for a more reliable schedule that would enable her to care for her aunt and her mother. While she no longer got choked up when the subject came up, she didn't like to talk about it, either. "I had some responsibilities that made a teaching schedule more workable—or so I thought. It didn't quite turn out that way."

A sudden look of recognition came over his face. "Oh. I hadn't even thought that you might have children. So you're married."

"Uh, no. No marriage. No children." How had their conversation taken such a sharp turn? He looked confused but said nothing, which led her to explain what she'd meant just to ease her discomfort. "The closest I ever got to marriage was a sort of fiancé, but... well, it seemed like a good time for a break." Realizing she was prattling on, she stopped talking.

Wes was apparently more comfortable with silence than she, for he studied her far too long before leaning back in his chair. "So you're sort of engaged but sort of taking a break."

Exactly. Rather than dig herself in any deeper, Emily left it at that.

He tilted his head and scrutinized her. "How long a break are we talking about?"

"That depends on my life expectancy." She wanted to call him *impertinent*, but that would make her sound schoolmarmish, so she'd resorted to snark.

He continued to stare with more interest than she expected. Feeling uneasy, Emily sprang to her feet. "I'll go get us some coffee." She escaped to the kitchenette in a flurry of nervous activity. "How do you take it?"

"Black."

"That's good. I don't have any milk." She'd meant to sound delightfully flippant but had failed miserably. Having regained her composure, she returned with two mugs and gave one to him.

He took it and wasted no time picking up where he'd left off. "What's his name?"

And there went her composure. "Uh..." All she could manage was a ridiculous frown.

The corner of his mouth moved just a bit. "You've forgotten already?"

"Oh, I remember, but I don't want to talk about it."

"Fair enough."

He was testing her, though she wasn't sure why. Even though she was flustered, he'd managed to draw more out of her than she would have volunteered. Emily wondered how this was going to work out. But for the sake of the lighthouse, she needed to try. No one else had volunteered to do what she could do, so she soldiered on.

"So, what did you have in mind for the campaign?" she asked.

He crossed his ankle over his opposite knee and leaned forward so closely that she could almost bury her nose in his hair and breathe in.

Wes launched into an impromptu plan. "I think a multipronged approach would be best. Our budget is modest, but we ought to have something in print for the locals, maybe a mailer that could also be posted in shops—and, of course, at the lighthouse itself. There's already a mailing list that the Friends of the Lighthouse have compiled from its visitors over the years, so we'll make use of that. There is a separate fundraising committee that will see to contacting wealthy patrons.

And the rest will be online—social-media ads, a landing page on the lighthouse website itself. The key is to make donating easy. The owner of our local computer shop has set all that up. So from you, I'll need a logo and some sort of graphic. It can be a photo, or it could be abstract. I'd love to see something that represents not only the lighthouse's past but its future as well." While he went on to talk about his vision of a nostalgic lighthouse with a modern twist, she multi-tasked—listening and identifying his scent, which she decided was lemon verbena mixed with a subtle hint of sea air and sand-dune grasses.

"Can you do any painting or photo manipulation?"

She gave him a look that said "Duh" in no uncertain terms.

His eyes sparkled and creased at the corners.

Emily began making plans. "I'll unpack my camera and go out in the morning. When I get back, say... in the late afternoon, we can go over some shots of the lighthouse together and take it from there."

"The best view—the one I think we should use—is from the water."

"Oh?"

"But you're the graphic designer."

She wasn't against his idea, but taking photos from the water would require a boat, which she neither had nor knew how to operate. But after running out of gas in front of his house, she wasn't about to mention that fact.

Oblivious to Emily's silence, Wes moved on with his plans. "Let's try a few angles and see what might work. I'll borrow a boat. Have you got all the camera lenses and filters you'll need?"

"Yes," she said with patience. He had no idea what she could do with a camera. *And why would he?*

"Good. All we need is to go on a shoot. You mentioned tomorrow?"

Maybe she'd grown too used to making deliberate decisions, but the way Wes could jump from one thing to the next made her head spin. Then again, why couldn't she go sailing the next day? Her calendar was pretty much clear for the next twelve months.

She shrugged. "Sure. That's fine. Tomorrow."

He talked more about the campaign. With no notes and probably little prior thought, he rattled off plans for a campaign that was sure to put the lighthouse issue in the forefront of everyone's minds. By the time he had finished, Emily was certain that, whatever his reasons for leaving the business, lack of talent was not one of them.

He stood up abruptly. "Okay. Well, I'll go see about getting us a boat, and I'll be back tomorrow. What time do you get up?"

"I don't know. It depends on whether I'm able to sleep." She wished she hadn't said that.

"Ah, a fellow insomniac. Well, do your best, because the view at dawn is amazing."

"Dawn?"

"You won't regret it. I promise."

Emily winced but nodded. "Well, okay. I guess I'll have to trust you."

"Smart woman. See you at six." He flashed a grin and was gone.

Emily blinked into the darkness outside her window. *Well, at least he isn't punctual.*

A knock sounded. Still a bit bleary-eyed, she opened the door. "Please don't tell me you're a morning person. I'm not ready for that."

His guilty smile confirmed her fears. "C'mon, sunshine. I'll buy you a coffee on the way." He held open the door.

Emily picked up her camera-gear backpack. "You know, I take better photos when I'm all caffeined up."

"We'll make that a priority, then."

By the time they were motoring out from the marina, Emily was seated with a hot coffee in hand, feeling wholly content. It was still shoulder season, so the only boats out were the fishing boats, most of which were long gone by that point.

Wes busied himself adjusting some of the lines then hoisted the mainsail and shut off the engine. Emily took the last sip of her coffee and held her face up to the morning sea breeze. The sun cast a warm glow through the mist.

"Look over there. That's your picture."

Emily lifted her camera and took a few dozen photos before the light changed. "Got it."

"Look at that shoreline. No matter how many times I've seen it, it's still different each time."

"There's something timeless about it."

Wes surveyed the site. "It's the way it looks out to the sea—simple and bold, defying the weather and the harshness of life." He laughed to himself as he glanced toward Emily. "Sorry. It's a bit early for me to start waxing poetic."

"How can you look at something like that and not be inspired?"

With a hint of surprise, he nodded. "I've got no time for anyone who can't."

Emily lifted her camera again and took more photos as they sailed back into the harbor. Wes secured the last dock line, and the two headed up the dock.

As a pair of men walked down the dock on the way to their boat, Wes touched Emily's shoulder and stepped back to let her go first, and they passed by the men in single file. It was a light touch, a meaningless gesture done out of courtesy. And it felt like a spark.

"Hungry?"

Still distracted by the feel of his hand on her shoulder, Emily looked up. "Yes, I guess I am."

"Good. We'll go to grab something to eat at The Anchor." He nodded in the direction of the only eating establishment in sight, a silvery cedar-shingled shack with a wall of windows that looked wearily out to the sea.

They made their way inside. A couple of weathered men sat at the bar and an older couple at a table by the window. The bartender waved an inviting hand toward the tables and told them to sit anywhere.

"Where to, madam?" Wes asked with a formality at odds with the bar's ambience.

Emily couldn't help but smile. "By the window?"

"Excellent choice."

They sat several tables away from the two other dining-room patrons, and Emily gazed at the harbor. She'd only just arrived, yet she wondered how she would ever be able to leave Hope Harbor at the end of her year here. Like fog that rolled gently in from the sea, it had enveloped her with a feeling of contentment she hadn't known in a very long time.

"I can't wait to see what you've captured with that camera of yours."

Pulled from her thoughts, Emily turned to Wes. "Oh, I left the camera in the car. I'll go get it." She was halfway out of her chair when he reached his hand out, touching her wrist.

He looked almost amused. "No, relax. I can look at them later."

Emily felt like she did on first dates: nervous. Which made no sense at all. They were working together and grabbing a quick bite to eat. How many times had she stopped to eat lunch with a colleague without reading anything into it? And yet there she was, feeling like someone who'd never talked to a man.

She forced her thoughts back on track. "I'll look through them and show you the best, and then I'll see what I can do with some digital painting."

"Sounds great."

The bartender came over and took their order. As he walked away, Emily turned to Wes. "So, advertising. I still can't quite see you in it."

"There's not much to see. I went to business school. My grades weren't stellar. But I went to a good school, wore a great suit to the interview, and managed to connect with the hiring manager on the topic of rowing, which I'd done in college. I'd like to say it was my first interview, but I'd been on seven before that. So basically, I went into advertising because advertising was the only field that seemed to want me."

In spite of his self-deprecating smile, his eyes held a distinct lack of amusement that Emily had noticed before when he spoke of his work. Ordinarily, she might have gone on to ask more, but every signal she picked up warned her that to do so would be a mistake. So instead, she asked about the lighthouse-restoration campaign, which kept them busy until their breakfast arrived.

By the time they'd finished, Wes had given Emily a very clear idea of the concept that he had in mind. She liked it, which surprised her, given some of the campaigns she'd worked on during her brief stint in the business world.

Wes leaned his arms on the table. "What is it about lighthouses?"

Emily thought for a moment. "I don't know. I suppose it's because they look alone but content. Yet at the same time, they're inviting. There are practical reasons of course. Their function invariably puts them out at the end of a landmass, in dangerous places. But in spite of the solitude, their light reaches out to the sea. Even though no one might see it, they're there just in case someone needs them. They save lives."

Wes's eyes softened. "I spent many summers here. And even as a boy, I felt a pull from the past. The lighthouse distills life to its essence, reminding us of what matters."

Emily nodded, agreeing. "Losing the lighthouse would be like cutting off part of history, like cutting off a tree at its roots."

"Exactly." His eyes lit up. "So how can we convey that with one picture? How can we portray the light-house as stemming from the past but reaching forward to the future?"

Emily leaned back and sighed. "Good question. I don't know if I have the answer, but I'll do my best to find it in the photos I took."

HOURS LATER, she was doing just that—staring at a computer screen full of thumbnails, searching for a picture with the feeling and message they hoped to convey. From time to time, she looked up and gazed through the window. She couldn't help it. She'd given up even trying to stop herself. Wes was out on the driveway again, tinkering with his old motorcycle, wearing worn jeans that defined every muscle and a worn-out T-shirt stretched over broad shoulders.

Emily leaned back in her chair and threw her arms in the air. *How's a girl supposed to work under these conditions?* With her mind still on Wes, she glanced at the screen and froze. Leaning forward, she clicked on an image. That was it. The light shone out to the water as though greeting the dawn while the lighthouse itself was nearly lost in the fog. The photo depicted a symbolic representation of the fate of the lighthouse as, no longer able to fulfill its duty, it would quietly fade from view until lost.

Without thinking, she ran to the door and called out to Wes. He dropped his wrench and ran to her cottage. He grabbed hold of her shoulders. "What's wrong? Are you hurt?"

Stunned by his concern, and even more by his touch, she looked into his eyes. "No, I'm fine."

He exhaled. "You scared me." As if waking up from a dream, he let go of her shoulders. "Sorry."

"No, I'm sorry. I, uh, sometimes get a little too passionate about my work."

Wes gazed into her eyes until a voice—hers—rescued the moment. "This photo. I think it's the one."

She sat down at the computer and adjusted the image to fill the full screen. "It still needs some work." She pointed out what she loved about it and what she planned to do with it. "I thought, with the light here and the sun—"

With his hand on the desk, Wes leaned over her shoulder. She turned to find his face inches from hers, and she stopped, having lost her train of thought.

His eyes were transfixed by the image. "That's it. It's perfect."

"I'm going to work with it a little and show you some options. I promise not to holler and scare you this time."

He drew his focus from the screen to her eyes. "Good work."

"Thanks. Just doing what I do." She inwardly cringed. She had just killed what was, for her anyway, a magical moment. *Just doing what I do—like an arrogant jerk?* She hadn't meant it that way, but who cared what she meant. Perception was what counted in the end.

To Emily's surprise, Wes didn't flee from her in revulsion. But that was probably a testament to his manners. "Well. See you later, then."

"Okay. Bye."

They parted ways at the door. Emily was leaning back against the door when a knock vibrated against her head. Still recovering, she turned and opened the door.

"How 'bout a working dinner? I'm thinking something fancy like pizza and wine."

Still staring, stunned, she said, "Sure." She looked at her watch. "I should have something to show you by seven or so."

"Good. I'll be back with pizza and wine about seven."

"Great."

Pizza and wine had never sounded so good. Emily glanced again at the time as she walked to the computer. She had a lot of work to do if she was going to have time for a shower and maybe makeup—not so much that he'd be able to tell, but just enough so she wouldn't look like she'd been up since the dawn of time.

FIVE

EMILY OPENED THE DOOR.

"Pizza delivery." Wes grinned as he stood at the threshold, holding a box of pizza in one hand and a bottle of wine in the other. He'd washed his hair and changed into a T-shirt without holes. He walked into the cottage and stopped dead in his tracks in front of the computer. He seemed to barely notice as Emily came over and relieved him of the pizza and wine.

After searching a bit through the drawer of utensils, Emily pulled out a corkscrew. "Ha! Found it!"

Wes turned to look at her as though he'd never seen her before. "This is perfect. Your design for the lighthouse says everything it should say."

Emily stood beside him and tried to view it from his perspective. "I don't know. I've been working all day on this, and I got to a point where I didn't know what else to do. So I thought I'd show it to you."

"Don't do a thing." He turned and gazed at her with a wonder that filled her heart with both joy and apprehension.

From the start, she'd tried so hard not to feel anything for him. She had tried to convince herself that this was just business. But what she felt now was so much more than that. "I was expecting a meeting with some sort of discussion. You're happy with this?"

An almost puzzled look came over him. "I'm sorry. I honestly thought we'd have more work to do, but you've done it. I hope you didn't think I came over on false pretenses."

"No, not at all. I'm glad that you like it."

"I love it. I wouldn't change a thing." He averted his eyes and then stiffened his posture. "Good work."

Only moments before, he'd gazed at her with as unguarded an expression as she'd ever seen from him. But something had shifted. His manner had turned guarded and formal so abruptly that he might as well have pushed her an arm's length away.

Emily did her best to hide her confusion. Hoping to lighten the mood, she said, "That just leaves more time for pizza and wine."

"Are you sure?"

"Sure that I'm hungry? Yes." A warmth spread

through her, and she smiled. "And thirsty. Yes on both counts."

That seemed to relax him a bit, or at least he stopped stealing glances toward the door. He followed her into the kitchen, where she poured two glasses of wine and got out plates for their pizza. They sat down at the table, and the awkwardness eventually lifted.

Midway through the meal, they'd exhausted their ideas for the lighthouse campaign, so Emily posed what she thought was a harmless enough question. "So, you used to work in advertising. You're so good at it. Why did you leave?"

"'Used to' is the best part of that sentence." He chuckled, but his amusement rang false.

Taking note, Emily leaned forward to ask more. As though he'd sensed what was coming, Wes stood up, took his plate to the sink, and started washing the dishes.

Emily made a note of how deftly he'd tried to distract her. Although she saw through the tactic, she refrained from pursuing the subject of his career track out of respect for his well-guarded privacy. She had to admit that doing dishes was an excellent means of distraction and possibly even more noteworthy than his job-related secrecy. If he didn't stop being so perfect, she might entertain thoughts of keeping him around.

Emily let him wash her plate while she refilled his

wine glass. "Would you like to sit out on the porch? I can't get enough of that view. But I think, even more than the view, the sound and the smell of the sea are... I don't know, therapeutic."

Wes opened the door and followed her outside. "I've solved nearly all the world's problems over there on my deck. And the ones that are left can't touch me there."

Emily leaned her head back against her chair. "What a wonderful place this must have been to grow up."

"I was only here in the summers, but yes. I had everything a child could dream of—happy family, great neighbors and friends. Although sometimes I wonder if it didn't set me up for later disappointment. The rest of the world isn't always so kind."

Emily hesitated to ask, but curiosity got the better of her. "That sounds like the start of the story."

"Maybe, but it's not one I'll bore you with now." His tone brightened. "Look how great everything looks in the moonlight. The moon must be close to full."

"Tomorrow," she said. He turned and scrutinized her. She shrugged. "It's on my Internet home page."

"And did your homepage tell you whether this might be a nice time for a walk on the beach?"

"No. I guess I'll have to decide that myself." She smiled and stood. "Come on. Let's go."

As they stepped off the porch, he took hold of her hand. There was something safe and unthreatening about the gesture. Over the last few years, Emily had built such a fortress around her own heart that she sometimes feared she would never remember how to let someone close. Maybe it was only the wine, but the moonlight, the waves on the beach, and her hand in his made her feel as if she might burst from holding in so much contentment. The feeling wasn't the same as the thrill of a crush or the hopefulness after a first date. She wasn't sure what it was yet. And that was the strangest thing about it—she didn't have to know where it was leading. He was holding her hand, a move that was simple and unencumbered by expectations, as though whatever their connection was meant to be would happen in its own time, and there was no rush.

When they got back to Emily's cottage, Wes stopped at the door and turned to face her. "I hope I'm not misreading signals." He lifted the hand he'd been holding and held it in both of his for a minute before gently lowering it to her side and releasing it. "We're working together, and that's what this dinner was for, so I don't want to presume."

"Presume?" *Have I voiced a complaint?*

"That there's something between us—I mean beyond business."

Now she was completely confused and a little

crestfallen. "Uh, no. I mean, I hold hands with all of my business colleagues."

He looked down and smiled. "Well, I guess I'm apologizing for that—unless you didn't mind it."

She peered into his eyes. "Look, Wes, I'm not really your type." *Girl, have you lost your mind?*

"My type?"

She couldn't tell whether he looked dismayed or annoyed. "Part of me will always be an artsy girl in black clothing and glasses, carrying a viola to school. I'm not flashy or sexy or anything like the women you're usually with—"

Ah, she knew that expression. It was irritation.

"How do you know that?" he asked. "What makes you such an expert on who I am?"

Emily leaned back and studied him. "Big man on your high school campus. Popular. Went off to an Ivy League school, where you hung out with your friends and unwittingly found yourself at the center of attention—from both men and women—because you're just you, and then you went on to a successful career in a high-profile ad firm."

He frowned then gave a couple of nods.

"I'm sorry. I—"

"No, don't be," he said. "You've nailed it. You've painted a vivid portrait of a narcissistic asshole."

"That's not what I meant. I just meant that I'm different. I'm not the type who appeals to..."

"A narcissistic asshole?"

"No. Ugh! You're twisting my words! I don't think that about you at all! I like you!" *Oh, great. Now why don't you ask him to go steady?* She wasn't thinking clearly. She'd come to Hope Harbor for a respite from the drama in her life, and she wasn't quite ready to feel what she was feeling for Wes. She hadn't expected any of this. She'd done such a good job of shutting down her emotions that these twinges of affection were painful. Yet she couldn't bring herself to avoid them—or him—or to even convince herself that she wanted to.

Wes lifted his eyebrows and took a step back, clutching his chest as if he'd been wounded. He was practically frowning, but his lips formed a hint of a smile. "So this is you liking me? You don't make it easy for a guy."

Emily's heart pounded so hard that she was afraid she was close to a panic attack. Why couldn't she have waited six months to meet him, or a year—or until she had her life back together and her emotions in check? She wasn't ready for this, but he was waiting for her.

It was her turn to speak, and she had to say something. "I'm sorry. I've had a lot going on in my life, and I..." *And what? Do you really think he wants to hear what's been going on in your life?* "Anyway, I'm just sorry."

"I wish you'd stop saying that." Wes leaned his shoulder against Emily's door and gazed into her eyes. "My takeaway from all that is that you like me. That's all I heard."

She thought that boyish grin of his would be her undoing, but then his deep-blue eyes settled on hers in a very unsettling way.

"And as I said, I don't want to presume anything," he said. "I just want to kiss you."

Emily averted her eyes. Until that moment, she had considered herself a well-balanced person. Sure, she was vulnerable, but she'd gone through the stages of grief and was well on her way to putting her life back in order. She was still of sound mind. But her hammering heart made her fear how she'd react to a kiss—to his kiss. She was already losing control. Kissing him would give life to feelings she'd been keeping in check, if just barely. She wasn't ready.

But when she dared look back into his eyes, logic flew out the window. "I want to kiss you too." That was her disembodied whisper she heard.

His eyes lit up as he smiled. "I'm glad to hear that. Truth is, you had me worried for a—"

Before he could finish his sentence, she kissed him. His lips were full and soft against hers. Then they parted. Maybe hers parted first. It all happened so fast. But he felt so good against her. She wanted to take him right there.

Then she stopped with a gasp just as quickly as she'd started, and she breathlessly whispered, "I'm sorry."

"For what?" He glanced about and exhaled.

"I didn't mean to—I mean I did, but I..." She shook her head, unable to speak anymore.

Wes took a step back as though he needed some distance to observe her, which he did with a crooked smile on the lips she'd just thoroughly kissed. He resumed the casual-leaning-against-the-doorframe posture that was suddenly looking way too appealing. "Don't apologize for a kiss—especially that one. 'Cause then I might have to feel guilty for enjoying it so much."

The warm smile on his face filled her heart, and she couldn't help but smile. "This is going to come as a big surprise, but I haven't been with anyone in a long time, except for my sort-of fiancé." She rolled her eyes and wrinkled her face. "He broke it off, but I wasn't expecting this." She noticed that his eyes were shining, and she realized her own eyes were probably star filled.

In a quiet, sure voice, he said, "It's okay."

That was it. No lengthy explanation about taking things slowly or defining what their relationship even was. It was simply okay. How he had accomplished that, she couldn't have said. But Emily felt a sense of peace for the first time in years.

Wes leaned down and kissed her on the cheek. "Let's go bicycling tomorrow. I've got some places I'd like to show you."

"Okay." Just as she began to feel comfortable, she realized a terrible flaw in the plan. "Oh. But I don't have a bike."

"No worries. We'll rent one in town."

"Okay." Emily did nothing to hide the beaming smile on her face. If he hadn't had the same foolish grin, she might have felt more self-conscious.

"I'll come pick you up at, say, nine o'clock in the morning."

"So I get to sleep in this time?"

"I knew you'd need time for coffee."

"You get me." She grinned.

He touched her shoulder then slipped his hand about her neck. He was bending down to kiss her when a car pulled into his driveway next door and triggered the motion-sensor floodlight. They both flinched and turned toward it like two teens whose parents had caught them kissing. Emily couldn't see who was inside the car, but something about the way Wes was staring prompted her to suspect that he knew both car and occupant.

"Were you expecting a visitor? I'm sorry. That was none of my business."

He gave her hand a squeeze and let go. "I've got to go. Thank you for, well, everything."

Emily nodded but couldn't seem to find the right words. She was about to take him inside, through her cottage, and out the front door, but he hopped over her porch rail and headed for home. As he disappeared from view, Emily went inside. She couldn't help herself—concealed by the shadows, she looked out the window, which was already open. There was no mistaking that it was a female voice greeting Wes. The two went inside, leaving what might happen next to Emily's imagination.

She poured some more wine and wondered why on earth she had let down her defenses. Why wouldn't there be women in his life? No one with his looks could spend much time alone.

She rolled her eyes. "Look at you—one little kiss, and your heart's all aflutter." Except it wasn't just one little kiss. It was a kiss like none she'd ever felt before and, depending on how things were going next door, might not ever feel again.

She got ready for bed and sipped some wine while she reread an old-favorite novel. Life was safe and predictable in those pages, and sometimes that wasn't such a bad thing.

"Vɪᴄ?" Wes called as he neared the driveway, although he knew who it was.

"Wes! I'm so sorry to show up like this."

"That's okay. What's happened?"

"Can we talk inside?" She was clearly upset.

"Sure." He opened the door and let her inside.

Only after the door was securely closed and locked did Vic speak. "I came here to warn you."

He offered her water, which she accepted, but she declined his invitation to sit. After she finished her water, she paced while she spoke.

"Sorry to be so cloak-and-dagger about it, but I found this in my apartment." She held up a small electronic device, and before he could ask, she nodded. "It's a bug. My daughter was playing, and she came up to me with that in her hand. 'What's this, Mommy?' I told her it went with my computer." She stopped pacing. "He sent people into my home— my parents' home, actually—and they touched things."

Wes leaned against the wall and folded his arms. "I wish I could say I'm surprised, but by now, I know better."

"I thought it was all over. That's why I'm here. I've got someone coming to sweep my apartment. I can't even believe I just said that. Anyway, I wanted to give you a heads-up without being overheard."

"Come here and sit down."

Reluctantly, she sat in a living-room side chair. Wes took a seat on the end of the sofa closest to her. "Where are the kids?"

She smiled gently. "Just like you to ask. They're with my parents." She leaned her head back and exhaled. "God, that feels good. I've been on pins and needles the whole way from Boston." She folded her legs up and wrapped her arms around her knees. "I'm so sorry. I should've known to expect it, I guess, but I had myself convinced it was over, you know?"

Wes shook his head. "One would hope."

"You know how it was."

Wes held up his palm. "Vic, you've got kids. They come first. I'm the one who told you not to testify, so why would I judge you?"

"I know." Tears filled her eyes, and she looked at him, shaking her head. "I'm all they've got."

In a calm voice, Wes said, "This is probably left over from before the trial. It makes sense that he'd want you to uphold the nondisclosure agreement—not that that gives him license to bug your home."

"Yes, that makes sense, except that I didn't move back in with my parents until after the trial. I've still got the settlement money, but I couldn't get a job.

When I realized Elliot had essentially blackballed me, my parents convinced me to move home so I could make my finances stretch until I'm working again."

"So Elliot bugged your home after the trial."

She nodded.

"Did something happen to prompt this?"

"Nothing. That's the thing."

Wes leaned back and stared at the ceiling. "But it's over. It doesn't make sense."

She leaned forward. "He's up to something. I know it. He already got what he wanted from me. I signed his settlement agreement. But you... watch your back."

Wes turned his gaze to her. "He's already done his worst to me—six months in jail. They can't retry me."

Victoria's eyes shimmered with tears. "I just can't stand the thought of anything more happening to you. You've been such a good friend."

Wes gave her a self-deprecating smirk, and she laughed. She glanced at her watch. "Oh wow, it's late. I'd better get going." She stood up and pulled her car keys from her pocket.

"It's too late to be out driving alone." Wes smiled his most charming smile. "That's a comfortable sofa. I'd sleep there myself, but my bed sheets are in bachelor condition. Trust me, you're better off here."

She shook her head. "You're so nice to offer, but I need to get back."

"But I was just going to make popcorn and watch costume dramas."

She laughed. "Oh, right!"

Wes laughed and waved his hand. "So quit arguing. I'll go get some bedding and sweats for you to sleep in—all clean, I promise, and the sofa is yours for the night."

EMILY THOUGHT about the swish of blond hair she'd caught sight of in the driveway floodlight when Wes left her cottage. There weren't too many reasons why a woman would show up at a man's home in the middle of the night. Emily could think of only one, so she hadn't slept well.

On her way to make coffee, she glanced out the window. Blond car girl was still there. So his friend had slept over. His *female* friend. Not that it was any business of hers. Except he had kissed her—or she had kissed him—just before his blond friend had arrived. That one kiss had changed things between them, at least in Emily's mind. And that was the problem. Had she only imagined the chemistry in that kiss? She was pretty sure she'd seen fireworks. But maybe he was just a really good kisser. Maybe it had meant nothing to him. Well, that was his choice, and hers was to stop allowing the chemistry between them to rule her emotions. She had let down her guard—which made her human, except for the fact that she'd done it with such ease and with so little thought.

Sometime close to nine, Emily's phone vibrated to announce a new text message. She finished the research article she'd been reading then took a look. She hadn't expected the message to be from Wes.

"Have to cancel our bike ride. Called out of town for a couple of days. Don't worry. I'll be back in time to present to the lighthouse committee. No need to prepare. I'll be ready, but they'll be sold when they see your design."

So that was it. A strange woman showed up on his doorstep, and anything that had started between them was over.

Emily muttered to herself, "It's probably nothing. They just spent the morning sipping coffee and watching the news. Like people do after spending the night together." She rolled her eyes and exhaled.

Determined to forget about Wes, she sat down to work on her dissertation. But every time she got up to refill her coffee, she couldn't help herself. She would glance toward his cottage to find that nothing had changed, until midmorning, when she looked outside and saw that the car in his driveway was gone.

Wes was gone and probably hadn't left alone. She

imagined them driving off, wearing sunglasses and smiles on their faces. Where they went didn't matter. It was somewhere happy—a place she hadn't been to in a while.

Had she imagined the mutual feeling between her and Wes? She thought back to the evening before. They had walked along the beach like people in a dating-app ad, holding hands. That had been Wes's idea. She would never have reached out to him. And it was his idea to kiss her. She didn't make that part up. He'd been about to say something to her when blond car girl arrived. It was probably for the best that he hadn't had a chance to say what was on his mind. Regardless of the chemistry between them, he had the same baggage everyone else had. And it looked like his baggage was blond. Emily wanted to hate her but knew that she was probably somebody special, because Wes was special. He deserved to be happy.

Emily deserved to be happy, too, so the sooner she forgot about him, the better off she would be. After all, they'd only just met, and she hadn't even been looking for this. She'd been perfectly—sort of—content before Wes. How hard could it be just to rewind to a few days back? No harder than putting toothpaste back into a tube.

SIX

WES WATCHED Vic's car turn the corner. He was weary. Any sleep he had gotten was fitful. He'd tried, but he couldn't think of how to explain Vic's sudden visit without telling Emily the whole story. He knew if he started, she'd never make it to the end of the story. Passing off the whole thing as a visit from a platonic friend was just not going to fly. It was the truth, but who would believe it? He might have managed to pull it off if Vic hadn't slept over. He'd basically ditched Emily and gone running to Vic. In his defense, Vic wouldn't have just shown up without a good reason. But that good reason stemmed from his criminal conviction. *Oh yeah, wait till she hears about that. Who doesn't love a guy with a record?* He had to face the cold truth about Emily: he had already lost her.

Even at that early point in their relationship, Wes knew without a doubt that Emily could have been someone special in his life. That didn't happen that much, at least not to him. He could think of one or two relationships that had felt like that from the start. But those thoughts were for romantic fools, which he was not.

He went to his mailbox and pulled out the morning paper. He loved the feel of newsprint on his fingers. No matter what life threw at him, he could still take pleasure in the simple act of sitting out on his deck, sipping coffee and reading the news. As he glanced at the headline, a car turned the corner and pulled up beside him.

A young, athletic guy leaned his head out of the window and smiled. "Wes? Wes Taggert?"

The guy seemed to recognize him, so Wes thought he had to be someone he'd known growing up. "Yeah?"

The man handed him an envelope. "Wes Taggert, this is a legal court document. The details are inside. Failure to respond could result in a default judgment against you. If you have any questions, please consult an attorney." Without waiting for a reaction, the man drove away.

Wes shut his eyes for a moment then turned and walked up his driveway and into his house. An hour later, he tossed a duffel bag into his trunk and drove off.

He'd already lost his friends, his reputation, and six months of freedom. Losing Emily would be an ache in his chest that he'd feel every time he looked at her and wondered what might have been.

THREE HOURS LATER, after a rush-hour drive that should have taken two hours, Wes sat across the desk from his lawyer with a bitter taste in his mouth. "My God, Mike. It wasn't enough that he put me through a criminal trial for assault. I spent six months in jail. My career's ruined. No woman will want to come near me. If it weren't for my trust fund, I'd be out on the streets —which, I'm guessing, must be his new goal."

His lawyer looked at Wes and did not disagree. "He knows what he's doing."

"Well, he's had enough practice. He's been harassing women for years, paying one off and then turning to another. But that wasn't enough. Now he's turned on me."

Mike Chadwick tilted back in his executive chair. "You know why. You apparently are the first person to try to stop him. He didn't know what to do about that."

"Well, he's figured it out—not once, but twice."

"We've got your back. I'm a criminal lawyer, so I've brought someone from our civil litigation department into the case, and not just any attorney, Kate's a senior partner. She's semiretired and doesn't take on many cases." Mike looked Wes straight in the eye. "You don't know how lucky you are yet, but you will."

The phone rang, and Mike picked it up. "Thanks." He pressed a button that was blinking. "Kate. How are you?" He was silent for a minute then said, "Do you mind if I put you on speaker?" He pressed a button. "Kate Rychter, I'd like you to meet Wes Taggert. He's the old friend of mine from college I told you about."

Kate said, "I'm sorry I couldn't be there in person."

Mike smiled. "No problem. I only gave you two hours' notice. Kate, we've talked about just the basics of Wes's legal scenario, but I thought you might like to hear Wes's side of the story."

"Absolutely. So, Wes, you say this was an ongoing pattern of behavior?"

Wes leaned forward. "Yes. It had gotten so bad that some of us in the office formed a sort of whisper network of past victims and fellow employees. We did our best to provide a buffer. We'd interrupt meetings at critical times. If he left orders to not be disturbed, we'd concoct bogus emergencies for the woman involved at the time, like a school nurse calling about a sick child or a spouse whose car had broken down and needed to be picked up—that sort of thing. One of the admins compiled a list of excuses and the dates we'd used them so we wouldn't repeat them too close together."

"And tell me about Victoria. I've read through the facts of the criminal case."

"Vic's a recent widow and single mom who was making ends meet while trying to be the best mom that she could be. And she was pretty. So it wasn't a surprise when Elliot started hitting on her. He'd done it before and really hurt some of his victims."

"Hurt them?" asked Kate.

"Mostly emotionally. But I suspect sometimes physically too. He had a way of making them think it was partly their fault for being there or dressing the way that they dressed, like they'd asked for it. It messed with their heads. There was one woman I cared for. By the time he was done with her, she left town. Last I heard, she was in therapy."

Kate spoke in calm, even tones. "And did anyone ever report him?"

Wes let out a bitter chuckle. "Elliot Lewis was nothing if not well connected. He had cronies looking out for him—including at least one judge."

Mike leaned forward. "We can't prove it."

"I hear you," said Kate. "And what about your relationship with...?"

"Vic—I mean, Victoria? It wasn't like that. We

were friends. Good friends—still are. But it was never like that. That was just one of the lies that he told to deflect attention from himself. That's how he always reacted when things would blow up. He would lie and then get his minions to swear to it. So he said I'd seduced her and that we were doing it all over the office—in the supply closet, the men's bathroom, under my desk—no doubt moves from his playbook, not mine. For me, there was no sex at work. Period."

"Tell me about the criminal case from your point of view. Mike will get me caught up on the details when I return."

"Lewis got to Vic before we went to court. She'd been out of work for a couple of months and had run out of money. So he offered to help her. His lawyer drew up an agreement with a nondisclosure clause. She hadn't filed anything against him yet, so her part could be brushed under the rug. The court case was his claim against me. So he presented the agreement to her, which included a large sum of money in exchange for her silence. No one blamed her, least of all me. She'd lost her husband, and she was holding it together for her children. The last thing she needed was to have her face in the papers and all over the news for her kids to see. She just wanted to get on with her life. She didn't know that they'd slipped in a nondisclosure agreement, barring her from discussing anything concerning her time with the ad firm. So she never testified in the criminal case."

Mike chimed in. "Kate, I tried to call her as a witness, but Wes was adamant. He wouldn't even try to get her to help us."

Wes chimed in. "Because doing so would have cost her the money she needed to live on, as well as her reputation. It would have ruined her and dragged her children down with her."

Mike nodded. He and Wes had been over this too many times. He turned back to the speakerphone. "So against the advice of counsel, Vic was kept out of it. As a result, there wasn't much of a case. The other witnesses who were still working there couldn't help without losing their jobs. I was able to find two past employees, but they had both signed similar agreements. It ended up being Elliot Lewis's word against Wes's. So Wes was sentenced to time served in jail and released with a criminal record."

The phone was quiet for a minute. "Okay. So, Wes, here's where we are. Of course I'll dig in and unearth every angle I can, but from what I've read and heard so far, it's not going to be easy without Victoria's testimony."

Wes shook his head. "Victoria is not in a good place

right now. She was sure that she'd get another job. She'd never had trouble before. But she'd never been blackballed by Elliot Lewis. She would interview, and it would go well. One time they even gave her the tax forms and new-hire paperwork then never called back."

Kate said, "Why do you think that is? If she'd signed the agreement, why wouldn't he just let her get on with her life?"

"Because he's a cruel bastard."

Kate said, "So he puts you through a criminal trial and makes you miserable and waits for the perfect time when your life has settled down. Then he hits you with a civil suit for maximum torture."

Mike nodded. "Exactly."

"You must have really pissed him off," said Kate. "I admire you for that. But I'm not gonna lie. We have a challenge before us. If Victoria can't or won't testify on your behalf, then—"

"I'm screwed?" Wes said.

"Well, we're going to do our best to see that doesn't happen. Nothing would give me greater pleasure than to find a way to keep your former boss from being able to screw anyone ever again. And I mean that both symbolically and—if wishes came true —literally."

Mike looked at Wes. "We've known each other

since college. You know that I'll do everything that I can to help Kate with this."

Wes nodded grimly. "You know, even now, I would do it again."

Kate said, "And that's why I asked to represent you."

Wes lifted his eyes with a questioning look, and Mike nodded, confirming.

Kate continued. "You're one of the good guys, and your old boss is one of the bastards."

Wes shared a smile with his friend. He had a good feeling about his new attorney.

"Your former boss has intimidated, assaulted, and probably raped more women than any of us would ever care to imagine. Your so-called assault isn't half of what that monster had coming to him."

Wes's mouth quirked at the corner. "That's not how the courts saw it. They seemed to think a broken nose, jaw, and two ribs were overkill."

Kate said, "It would give me great pleasure to finish the job."

Wes couldn't help but smile, because he knew she meant it.

"Let me ask you something." Kate paused. "What would've happened if you hadn't done what you did?"

Anger roiled up inside Wes. "When I broke down the door, he had her pinned to the couch. When I told him to get off her, his pants were unzipped. He was going to rape her."

"Well, okay, then. I'll be back in town Wednesday, and then we'll get to work."

Mike ended the call and turned to Wes. "See what I mean? She's got this."

SEVEN

EMILY HAD WASTED a day feeling sorry for herself. Wes was gone, so enough was enough. She went into town to buy groceries and a few extra items to pamper herself. As she walked into a diner for a preshopping lunch, she decided, as pampering went, she was easy to please. What made her glance at the newspaper dispenser, she couldn't have said. She read all of her news online lately. But she did glance, and there he was on the front page. The caption read, "Disgruntled Boss Beater Soon Back in Court." She bought a copy just as a waiter signaled for her to follow him.

She slipped into a booth and pored over the article, trying not to feel sick to her stomach. How could this be the same man? Deemed too violent to be set free on bail, he'd spent six months in jail. The article painted a picture of a man with wild, uncontrollable rages who'd formed an obsession with a woman at work. One day, while the woman in question was in a business meeting with their boss, Wes Taggert stormed in and assaulted the man. The attack was so brutal that Elliot Lewis spent the following week in the hospital, recovering from a concussion, a broken nose, and two cracked ribs.

Emily's food arrived, but she'd lost her appetite. She asked for it to be wrapped up to go, and she hastily left for a quick trip to the grocery store and then home.

As soon as she'd unpacked the groceries, she sat down at the computer for a long afternoon to research the matter. Wes had worked at a prestigious advertising firm. According to the testimony, he and the female employee had embarked on a relationship that flew in the face of the company policy. One witness testified that the pair's office behavior had grown so flagrant that he'd found them in the supply closet together and then in a men's bathroom stall. Action was taken. As a result, she broke it off, and he became obsessed with her. When Wes got wind of a meeting their boss had arranged with the woman, Wes tried to barge in, but the door was locked. He heard moaning inside and he flew into a rage, eventually breaking open the office door. Once inside, he pulled his boss from his chair and repeatedly pounded him with his fists. The boss was older and unable to defend himself against Wes's superior strength, but that didn't stop Wes from continuing the brutal pounding. By that time, Elliot Lewis's administrative assistant had called security. It took two men to pull Wes away. Minutes later, the police arrived and arrested him. In the end, the judge sentenced Wes to six months' time served.

Emily got up and paced the floor for a minute, glancing over at Wes's cottage from time to time, stunned. How could that be the same Wes that she knew? She couldn't believe she'd spent time alone with a man who was capable of that sort of violence. And he'd never mentioned anything about being in jail. Of course not. Why would he? People didn't just come out and say, "Oh, by the way, have I mentioned that I spent six months in jail because I was convicted of an assault that put a man in the hospital for a week? Oh, and are you busy Friday? How 'bout pizza?"

She felt like such a fool for believing that he'd left the dog-eat-dog business world to get back to nature. Her need to escape her own life had made it easy for her to think he might want the same thing. Instead, he'd escaped the life that he'd ruined and the people who knew what he'd done. People in Hope Harbor had known him since childhood. They had to have heard what had happened. Boston wasn't that far away, and bad news did travel fast. But the Wes she knew had helped her. Except for the motorcycle, he was quiet and stuck to himself. But wasn't that what they always said about men who one day went berserk and turned violent?

Emily had nearly walked into a dangerous mess—not to mention that Wes's unhealthy prior relationship might not have ended yet. After reading the article, she still couldn't believe it was the same Wes. But even if he had a reasonable explanation, how could she believe it? To do so would be to gamble that he wouldn't become violent toward her, and that was too great a risk. Emily had dodged a bullet.

EMILY LOOKED AT HER WATCH. She'd been on this bench in the lobby of the community center for ten minutes that felt more like twenty. She'd arrived early and waited to the uneven rhythm of footsteps on the old wooden floor. She'd been uneasy enough about seeing Wes and didn't want to add a last-minute rush to the mix. Even so, after having three days to relive and overthink what had happened, she'd had ample time to rehearse an air of poise that she did not possess.

Wes rushed in. "Sorry. Am I late?"

"No, just in time, actually." She would not be distracted by how good he looked. His hair was neatly drawn back, and his beard was trimmed to a stylish stubble that just drew focus to his strong cheekbones.

His new T-shirt was dressed up by a sports coat and jeans. But when he bent down and touched his lips to her cheek with the lightest of kisses, she caught a good whiff of man scent. Part of her was inclined to go to the nearest department store and smell every bottle behind the glass counter until she found this one. Then the smart part of her shuddered. *Disconcerted* did not even come close to describing how she already felt, but then he looked into her eyes, and she got stupid again. She felt as if a sun god—it didn't matter which one—had just smiled upon her, and she started to trust him all over again. *Emily, look at yourself.* Why couldn't she just believe what she'd read in the news?

She was too attracted to Wes not to have seen the inevitable attraction coming, so she'd prepared herself for that gaping point of weakness. Every time she thought chemistry might roil to the surface and take her mind hostage, she imagined the shadow of Norman Bates in *Psycho*. Of course, that tactic was going to wreak havoc with her showering schedule, but she'd worry about that later.

Wes probably had no idea of what she'd discovered about his past or how adamant she was to make sure this thing was over before it started.

"Do I look okay?"

"Yes, you look great." Emily forced herself to maintain her composure when he flashed a confident smile.

"Would you like to begin?"

Emily quickly said, "No, thank you. I'll just fill in if needed."

Wes grinned. "Sounds like a plan."

A committee member appeared in the doorway. "Ready?"

Emily lifted her chin and smiled. "Yes, we are."

AN HOUR LATER, they emerged from the meeting room with huge smiles on their faces, but they didn't say a word until they were safely outside, out of earshot.

"What was that?" she asked, still feeling a little shocked.

"What was what?" He looked genuinely confused.

"Or should I say, who was that? You were so... I don't know. I want to say *slick*, but not in a slimy way."

"Thanks?"

"But you just owned the room." A hank of hair had come loose during the presentation and now hung over his face. It was driving her mad—it looked so good on him. She could hardly keep from touching it.

"Co-owned it. You looked completely in control, and comfortable speaking in front of people."

"Well, I do teach for a living, so I'm not unaccustomed to speaking in public, but I'm much more comfortable doing art."

He was beaming. "Once you pulled out your design for the campaign, that was it. It was over."

"Before you get too excited about my artistic genius, don't forget that they had no one else to choose from."

Wes reluctantly nodded. "But without you, they'd have been forced to go to an ad agency, and that would have cost them. So this is huge."

Now he's just being kind. "I suppose."

"You suppose that I'm right? Good call." He grinned, and his face lit up. "Let's go celebrate. I'm buying. Your car or mine?" He put his hand on her back and started to take a step forward, but Emily held her ground.

She'd come close to convincing herself not to like him, but she hadn't anticipated how seeing him again would send her good sense out the window. Even with her judgment impaired, she remembered that getting into a car with a convicted criminal was not in her life plan, so before she weakened further, she blurted out, "No."

"No?"

"I'm sorry. I can't." She averted her eyes, unable to face that expression. He looked stunned, as if he'd been struck and knew something was wrong but hadn't fully processed it yet. This was the moment she'd dreaded. Bracing herself, she looked into his eyes. "I think we should keep this all business."

He frowned but recovered and nodded as though he understood.

Uncomfortable with Wes's silence, Emily pressed on. "I love working together, but I'm just not looking for anything else."

"Right." He peered at her for a moment. "Okay." His face transformed to what she guessed was his positive, businesslike expression. "Well, good night, then." He set off for his car while she reminded herself why it was better this way.

EMILY WAS on her way back from a morning walk along the beach when she caught sight of Wes working on his motorcycle. He glanced in her direction, but she was still far enough away to be able to pretend there had been no eye contact. But she saw a change in his posture and the tilt of his head—or maybe her guilt for dumping him so abruptly was making her imagine it. She had done the right thing by brushing him off, but as she approached her house, she kept remembering the pain in his face.

A voice from behind called out, "I thought that was you."

Emily turned to find Delia heading her way. After they exchanged hellos, she invited Delia to sit down on the back porch. She went inside, poured two glasses of iced tea, and brought them out to where Delia sat.

"So, you seem to be all settled in." Delia took a quick sip of her tea.

Emily smiled warmly. "I am completely unpacked, and I'm thoroughly enjoying the cottage."

A loud clanking sound came from the driveway next door. Delia called out to Wes, "Are you okay?"

"Fine. I just dropped this old wrench. It's lucky. It deserved so much worse than that."

Delia laughed. "Just take care of yourself!"

"Yes, Miss Langdon," he said in the tone of an obsequious schoolboy.

Delia was still smiling when she turned back to Emily. "You couldn't find a better neighbor than Wes."

Emily wasn't sure what to say. The obvious response would be to agree, but knowing what she'd read about Wes, she didn't feel comfortable doing that. So she opted for silence.

"Oh, that reminds me. Everyone's raving about your designs and Wes's plans for the lighthouse-restoration campaign." She leaned closer conspiratorially. "You two make a good team."

Emily let out a nervous laugh. "It worked out well that we both have skills to contribute to the cause."

Delia gave her a knowing look. "And who knows what other skills Wes might have to offer."

"Delia, if I didn't know better, I'd think you were trying to play matchmaker."

Delia leaned her head back in the chair and laughed. "I honestly don't usually do this, but there's something about you and Wes that just makes me want to see the two of you together."

Emily smiled patiently. "It's a nice thought, but I don't think he's my type."

Delia barely turned as she lifted an eyebrow. "Dear girl, that man is everyone's type." Her smile faded, and an earnest expression took its place. "But seriously, he's more than just a pretty face. He's a kind and honorable man."

Emily didn't feel it was her place to disabuse Delia of that notion, but if her landlady didn't let this go, she was going to have to say something.

Delia's face brightened. "Oh, I nearly forgot why I chased you down. I've been wanting to cook. Are you busy Saturday?"

Emily's calendar was practically clear for the next several months, it so happened. "Saturday? No, I'm not busy."

"Why don't you plan on coming over around

seven? I'll cook us some dinner and maybe make margaritas."

"That sounds great. I look forward to it."

"Good. See you then."

As Emily headed for the door, Delia held her hand up. "Don't bother. I'll just go out this way. I want to say a quick hello to your neighbor." She stepped off the porch and along the side of the cottage.

Emily watched Delia head straight for Wes. Delia didn't seem like the type who didn't read the news. Still, she had the right to not know all the world's troubles. Emily stole a glance at Delia and Wes then went inside and got back to work.

EIGHT

Emily poured herself into her work, relying on her powers of concentration to keep her mind off of Wes. That was something she'd done for a number of years when she'd lived a sort of tunnel-vision existence, blocking everything out but the most immediate concerns. In some ways, that was easier than living a normal life—if there was such a thing. At least during her workday she'd had some sort of human interaction. But in her seaside cottage, she found herself feeling very alone, which felt strange since she'd wished for alone time on so many occasions—or maybe she'd only longed for a respite from responsibility.

After two days buried in work, she looked forward to dinner at Delia's. Spending time with female friends was something she'd cut out of her life to make room for her caregiving duties. The simple act of being with someone she could share a drink with, and maybe laughter, with no expectations but friendship seemed inviting. With that in mind, Emily showered and threw on a comfortable shirt and a pair of worn jeans. With her hair brushed back into a loose ponytail, she headed down the road toward Delia's house.

Delia, it turned out, lived in a beautiful home. It was far larger on the inside than one would expect from the look of the front. Even more surprising was how modern it was. Delia didn't have to explain that it had been recently renovated. Everything had the stamp of minimalist taste and high quality, from the gleaming wood floors to the white-planked walls and beams overhead. After chatting their way through a tour from the front door to the kitchen, Emily stopped in her tracks.

Wes turned from the counter with a newly poured drink in his hand and a deer-in-the-headlights expression. He quickly recovered and smiled. "Hello." It was clear he'd had no more idea than she that they'd both be at Delia's.

"Wes. Hello." She glanced at Delia, not even trying to hide her silent accusation.

Delia's eyes opened in an apparent attempt to look innocent. "Oh, didn't I mention I'd invited you both?" She looked down at the avocado she'd just begun peeling.

Emily wanted to say, *No, you did not*, in no uncertain terms. Instead, she did her best to rally. With some semblance of poise, she turned back to Wes. "How are you?"

"Fine, thank you. And you?" His reply was flawlessly well-mannered, but his narrowing eyes hinted at the frown he had failed to suppress.

"Oh, I'm fine." Emily smiled politely, and their eyes locked. It appeared they had arrived at the end of the mannerly portion of the conversation, and neither seemed to know where to go next.

Delia mercifully broke into the awkwardness. "Excuse me a minute." Then she disappeared.

When the door closed behind her, they both started talking at once, then both stopped. Wes smiled. "You go first."

Emily glanced nervously in the direction of where Delia had just disappeared. "I, uh, I can't remember what I was going to say."

There was something different in his gaze, something penetrating, as though he saw through her. What he said next confirmed it. "I gather you've seen the newspapers."

She opened her mouth to protest, but how could she when he was right? She just offered a feeble shrug.

"It's not how it looks, but I know how that sounds,

so I won't trouble you with my side of the story. I just don't want to see that look in your eyes."

"I don't know what you mean." She knew exactly what he meant. She couldn't even look him in the eye.

"I see fear—like you're worried I might suddenly fly off the handle and..." He looked away then turned back to face her. "Look, I don't care what you think of me. Well, actually, I do, but it's a little too late for that. I just want you to know that I would never hurt you. Ever."

She had never seen anyone look so sincere—or so hurt—and she desperately wanted to believe him. But that was the trap. What if he was one of those men who seemed perfectly nice until a switch flipped, and he went into a rage? Her gut feeling might say to trust him, but logic had to rule here.

Delia breezed into the kitchen, brandishing two limes. "They must've rolled out of the grocery bag and onto my car floor. I found them hiding under the seat. Now I can make us some proper margaritas." Delia refused Emily's offer of help and, instead, shooed them away while she busied herself with the meal preparations. "Why don't you two go and relax on the porch? There's a full moon tonight, so it's gorgeous out there."

Just what I want—to be under a full moon with Wes Taggert. What had possessed Delia to do this to them? If he started to howl, she was heading home.

Out they went, because Delia had said to and neither of them was about to go against Delia's wishes. Wes's eyes shone with adoration and respect as if he were still twelve years old and taking payment for mowing her lawn. For Emily, Delia was the first friend that she'd made in a long while, and she treasured the few friendships she had.

Once outside, Emily sat on the far side of a picnic table, facing out to the sea. The moon shed its light over a shimmering ocean. She was horrible at conversation even in the best of circumstances. As each moment grew more awkward, she couldn't even bring herself to look at him.

"Well, she's right. That's a very full moon." Wes sat down beside her and looked out to the dunes.

"The paper said you assaulted your boss." She couldn't believe she'd just blurted it out. But he was sitting so close, and it made her too tense to pretend to make small talk.

His sharp glance struck its target. "I did."

Emily hadn't realized how much she'd wanted him to deny it until he'd openly admitted it to her. She stood up to escape the silence that followed. She went to the edge of the porch, where she leaned against a pillar. "I'm sorry. It's none of my business. I couldn't help but wonder. I just didn't expect it to be true."

"Understood. But we've got a whole evening ahead

of us, and Delia's gone to some trouble. So let's not disappoint her. The woman's a saint."

"Chips and guacamole, anyone?" Delia brought a platter and napkins and set them on the table. Then she stopped and stared at the moon. "How lucky are we to have a view like that to look at whenever we want?" As she sat down to join them, she glanced at Emily, then her gaze settled on Wes, and a look was exchanged.

Wes excused himself and headed inside.

Delia called after him. "Down the hall on the left." She watched him disappear through the doorway then turned to Emily. "I want to see him happy. He deserves it."

Emily turned and leaned her back against the post, facing Delia. "Does he?"

Delia smiled. "So do you." Her wise gaze bored through to Emily's conscience until she felt the need to explain.

"He's not for me, Delia." As Emily heard herself say those words, she felt a pang in her chest. She glanced over and saw Wes in the doorway. She didn't need to wonder how long he'd been standing there. His face said it all.

Delia watched the two of them frozen in a moment of uncomfortable silence. She spoke in a tone that was both bright and casual. "It's a funny thing. I've been around long enough to remember when news was reported objectively. I'm sad to see those days gone. Now everyone has their own angle. It's hard to know what's true anymore."

Wes regained his casual bearing and sauntered over to sit beside Delia. "I can tell you one thing that's true. You make a great margarita."

Delia's light laughter eased some of the tension. "I'll tell you my secret. If you put enough tequila in the blender, it tastes good sooner or later. That's also the secret to my cooking. Speaking of which, I'd better go check on dinner."

"I'll come help." Emily started to follow, but Delia waved her away. "Sit down. I've got it."

Emily watched Delia leave. "Well, she's not subtle, that's for sure."

Wes nearly smiled. "She likes things to be the way they should be—like the lighthouse. And she's not afraid to work to make sure that it happens."

Emily's eyes widened. "Well, she seems to have made us a project."

Wes fixed his gaze on Emily. "She likes us both, and she wants us to be happy. Delia saw me through a tough time. So now I think her innate sense of fairness drives her to make things right for me. Unfortunately, she's got this crazy idea that you're the one who could make that happen." He took a last drink from his glass and muttered, "I did too, actually." He got up and reached for the pitcher, refilled both their glasses, then sank into a chair. "So, Miss Emily Cooke, we've got a dinner to get through this evening. Let's pretend to enjoy it for Delia's sake."

For some reason that she could not understand, she felt guilty. She'd done nothing wrong. In fact, she'd done everything right. A single woman had to look out for herself. Spending quality time with a man who had been convicted of assault had never been on the agenda. The worst part was, everything she saw in Wes contradicted what she'd read about him. There had to be more to the story, but would learning it just send her deeper into a heartbreaking situation?

Delia announced that dinner was ready, and the two guests behaved amicably as Wes had suggested. Fortunately, Delia made it easy. They got on the topic of her travels. With anyone else, that might have spelled doom for the evening, but Delia clearly enjoyed sharing tales of her travels, and they were fascinating. After dinner, she pulled out her photo albums. She had, in fact, been to some spectacular places, with stories to tell that were all the more interesting because she had traveled alone. Emily found herself admiring Delia more and more as she got to know her. By the end of the evening, she'd almost forgotten her discomfort with Wes.

Emily stayed to help finish the dishes. She was hoping Wes would head for home at that point. In the previous century, her plan might have worked, but Wes washed while she dried, and Delia put it all away. The time came when they were finished, and Emily had to face the walk home. Common sense told her to go alone, but she didn't know how to manage that without making things awkward. Delia solved her dilemma by coming right out and asking Wes if he'd walk Emily home. She'd feared that might happen, but she still hadn't managed to devise a way out. She considered her options. In the time she'd known Wes, he'd been unerringly polite. That, combined with Delia's unwavering faith in him, prompted her to agree. She still felt uneasy, but pressing the issue would have made things even worse. Besides, even if she did manage to slip away all alone, what was to stop Wes from catching up with her along the way? The man lived right next door. He knew where to find her, so walking home with him was no more risky than being home alone. That realization was the most unsettling of all. She made a mental note to go into town the next day and get materials to replace the door locks.

Since the walk home was apparently going to happen, Emily turned to Delia. "I'll text you when I get home. If you don't hear from me, please call the police." She said it with a little laugh at the end to lighten its effect. However, from the corner of her eye, she caught a sharp look from Wes. The two guests thanked Delia and said their goodbyes, then they headed outside for home.

THE FULL MOON lit their way down the stone path to the road, then Wes and Emily turned toward their houses. When they were well out of earshot of Delia, Wes said, "I imagine there's nothing I can do to put you at ease."

Of course, that put Emily even less at ease. She kept her eyes straight ahead. "Delia trusts you, so I'm trusting her."

They walked another few steps in silence, then Wes said with no warning, "My parents were in Florida when this whole thing blew up." He lifted his eyes to meet hers. "The assault. My father had a heart attack on the day he heard the news."

Emily took in a breath, but Wes interrupted before she could speak. "He's okay now. But at the time, he couldn't be moved, and he needed my mother there with him. Delia looked after me. She stopped by the cottage almost daily. She'd pretend that she'd been out for a walk, but I knew what she was doing. Then when I was arrested, she came to visit me..." He hesitated. "In jail." He glanced over at Emily with a crooked grin. "I think she'd have baked a cake with a file in it if I'd asked her."

Emily smiled at his attempt to lighten the mood, but inside, her natural tendency to empathize warred with her apprehension.

As they reached Emily's cottage, Wes stopped on the road by the walk that led up to the cottage. "Look, I get it. We spent some time together. We had a nice time—at least I did. Then you read in the paper that I'm some kind of monster."

She opened her mouth to protest.

He lifted his hand, interrupting. "No, I understand. What else would you think? I don't blame you at all."

Emily looked in his eyes. She didn't care if the full moon revealed the full force of her resentment. "There's one thing I just don't understand. When were you going to tell me?"

"I don't know. This thing took me by surprise."

"This thing?"

"You... us. I didn't know what was happening until it had already begun. Or maybe I just wanted to pretend you could care for me."

She almost told him she did. That would have been a mistake.

"But I knew. When it started to look like there was

going to be something between us, I knew that I'd have to tell you. By then, I realized it would hurt you, and I knew it would hurt me. So I put it off as long as I could. I honestly planned to tell you on the day we went biking together."

"Which we never did."

He looked down and shook his head.

Emily filled in the next part. "Because you had a visitor."

Wes shoved his hands in his pockets and stared at the pavement. "I know that I keep saying this, but it's not what you think."

"The thing is, I don't want to think. I wasn't looking for this. Even without the newspaper reports, there's a mountain of baggage between us—not all yours. I've got my own."

"Everyone has baggage. I'd like to think we could work through all that."

"It sounds nice, but the truth is, we hardly know each other. And I'm not up to the task. What you've done in the past, who your overnight guests are—it's none of my business. I never had any claim on you. This isn't me being jealous. This is me letting go." She turned, walked up the path to her front door, and went inside without looking back.

NINE

Wᴇꜱ ᴡᴀꜱ ᴜᴘ ᴀᴛ ᴅᴀʏʙʀᴇᴀᴋ, working on his motorcycle. Lately, it was the only thing that took him away from his troubles. When he wasn't busy with his bike, his thoughts were consumed by the lawsuit. He'd been here before. Although his current situation wasn't as bad as giving up his freedom for prison, his career had been ruined. No one would hire him, thanks to Elliot Lewis. Even so, he was luckier than most would be in his position. His grandfather had left him a trust that he used to view as his emergency fund. Now it was his sole means of support. It wasn't a lot, but thanks to Delia, who charged him a fraction of what she could get in rent, it was enough to live on.

In that way she had of contriving coincidences, Delia happened along on an afternoon stroll. "So, how are you?"

"Okay."

"And the case?"

He put down his tools and stood to give her a recap of his meetings with the lawyers.

"Good. It sounds promising." She studied him. "You sure you're okay?" She had a way of looking into his eyes that kept him from being able to tell her anything but the truth.

"I've been better. But as you know, I've been worse. So I know this will end. I just hope it will end with some of my finances intact."

Delia stared down the road with a thoughtful expression. "Wouldn't all this go away if the witness to the assault testified on your behalf?"

Wes shook his head. "I refused to do that to her during the criminal trial, so why would I do that now?"

"But how can she do that to you? I've never under-stood it. I'm sorry. I know that you think she's your friend, but it just isn't right to put you through all this."

"Victoria's been through enough. She's a widow with two kids to support. She's lost her job, and no one will hire her, thanks to Elliot. So when he presented her with a nondisclosure agreement, I urged her to sign it for the money. He'd hurt her enough. I saw no need to put her through any more. Nothing has changed as far as she is concerned. If she testified at the civil trial, she'd break the agreement and have to give back all the money he paid her. It's okay. I'll get through it."

Delia gave him that gentle smile that always made him feel as if he were ten years old again, being fed milk and cookies. "You're a good man."

Wes discounted her praise with a shrug. As Delia smiled and shook her head at his humility, she glanced over at Emily's cottage. "How are things with you two?"

"Emily?" Of course he knew who she meant, but it was a stalling technique. He wished he had a stalling technique that would last longer than fifteen seconds. He glanced at his bike. The conversation was taking an uncomfortable turn. "I'm sure Emily's as fine as I am. We're just not fine *together*." He put on his most charming look of mock reproach. "Although it's not for your want of trying. There were times during dinner the other evening when I thought a road-company production of *Fiddler on the Roof* was in town."

Her eyes twinkled as she smiled with pride. "Thank you. I think I'd make a very good matchmaker. I certainly know two people who belong together when I see them."

Wes's attempt at charm was nothing compared to Delia's superior skills at persuasion, but he would not yield. He smoothed back his hair and lifted his eyes to meet hers. "Not gonna happen."

"It would if you'd tell her the truth. Frankly, it's all I can do not to tell her myself."

Wes took in a sharp breath.

Before he could protest, Delia said, "Don't worry. I won't. That's your truth to tell. But it's hard to stand here and watch you making a terrible mistake."

Wes clenched his jaw.

Delia looked up at him with heartfelt concern. "What is it? I don't understand."

Wes took a moment to get his emotions in check. "She didn't trust me. We'd spent time together. She knew who I was. But the first time doubt was raised, she believed it. I didn't see any point after that."

Delia trod carefully. "She's not a mind reader, Wes."

"Mind reading has nothing to do with it. She should have believed in me, no matter what. That's what people do when there's something between them —something I thought we had." He shrugged. "Look, it's all water under the bridge. I've got a lot of work to do on this bike before it gets dark."

Delia nodded. "All right. I'll let you off the hook this time." Her eyes softened. "If you need anything, you know where to find me."

Wes gave her a hug then headed up the driveway and got back to work. But it wasn't the same. He could no longer escape all the worries that plagued him. Not only the lawsuit dominated his thoughts, but now Emily did as well. What if Delia was right? What if he had expected too much? After all, they'd only known each other for two or three weeks. It felt like so much longer—maybe just to him. His feelings for her had grown so strong that perhaps he had assumed far too much on her part.

Unable to work anymore, Wes put bike and tools back inside the garage. All this would make much more sense after a beer. So he headed inside.

Emily sat on the public bench outside of the light-house, allowing the sea breeze to wash over her senses. But her thoughts persevered, unrelenting as the waves in their constant assault of the shoreline. This was so unlike her. She'd grown expert at holding her emotions at bay, because she had good sense, or she used to. She'd lost all of it, and in Hope Harbor of all places— the place she had come to regain some control over her life. Instead, the control she so longed for was slipping away.

Footsteps approached. She kept her eyes fixed on the distant horizon, hoping that whoever it was would walk on and leave her alone. But the footsteps stopped by the bench. She looked up to find Wes holding out a to-go cup of coffee.

Emily couldn't help but smile as she took it. "You've got me figured out, haven't you?"

"At least where mornings and coffee are concerned. I remember from the day we went sailing."

Of course he remembered her penchant for coffee, because that was what thoughtful people did. It was the sort of thing she did for others. But no one had ever done it for her. She inwardly sighed. Why wouldn't he just make it easy to distance herself from him? "How did you know where to find me?"

He leaned back and crossed his ankles. "I didn't exactly. But I've seen you return from your walks in the mornings. I'm not stalking you, just so you know. I have my own habits. I happen to sit on my back deck every morning, drinking my coffee, about the same time you go on your walks."

She nodded and cast a sideways glance. "I know. I've seen you. I just didn't want it to look like I was checking you out."

Wes lifted an eyebrow. "But you were. Good to know."

"I wasn't—so don't let it go to your head." She looked into his eyes and felt sudden dread for what she was going to say as soon as she got the courage.

He slumped back against the bench. "Oh, I don't

think I'm in danger of having anything go to my head as long as I'm with you." He flashed a grin, but it faded when he saw the look on her face. "What?"

The water reflected the morning sun in a thousand shimmering flickers of light. It was going to be one of those beautiful days by the sea, the sort of day that should have no regrets. And she was about to ruin it. She began in a quiet, apologetic tone. "I like you."

"Oh, shit."

She turned quickly, thinking something had happened. Maybe he'd spilled his hot coffee on his lap, or something else—anything else but her. But his gaze was steady, if stunned. "What's wrong?" she asked.

"I don't know, but I think I'm about to find out."

She said, "Whatever you're thinking, you're wrong."

"Oh, I don't know. I'm thinking I shouldn't have come looking for you."

She could not quite agree, but she couldn't help being curious. "Why did you?"

Wes shifted his weight and rested his arm on the back of the bench, inches from her shoulder. "Delia and I had a talk. Apparently, I haven't been fair to you."

That took Emily by surprise. "Oh?"

"I haven't quite told you the truth about me, at least not all of it."

Emily tried not to frown. "If this is another one of Delia's attempts to get us together, I wouldn't take it as a reason to... uh... what I mean is, you don't owe me anything."

"I need to tell you the truth."

"Wes..." She felt like she shouldn't want to hear it. Continuing to talk about it just postponed the inevitable. It was time to let go. Yet she listened.

"I'm not the horrible person the newspapers would have you believe. I was protecting someone."

"Your overnight houseguest?"

His eyes narrowed. "Vic? Well, yes, but not the way that you're thinking. We weren't together. It wasn't like that."

"Okay. So you helped her. You did the right thing. Delia thinks way too highly of you for there not to have been a good reason. So now I know you're a good guy. I respect you for it, but nothing has changed where you and I are concerned."

He brushed back a few strands of hair that the sea breeze was having its way with. "Man, I read this so wrong. I thought we had... something." He turned to her. "Look, it's okay. I just thought we connected. I thought there was... I don't know, more than this."

Emily turned and looked into his eyes, and she felt that connection. She'd felt it before, but this time it made her heart ache. The least she could do was tell him the truth. "That's the problem. There's too much. I just can't." She couldn't look at him anymore. Her emotions were too close to the surface.

"Look, Em..."

He'd called her that a few times when they'd worked on the lighthouse campaign. No one else called her that, and it made her heart swell every time that he said it. The nickname itself wasn't so magical, but it was between them and nobody else. It seemed a bit foolish to have such a reaction, but there were feelings between them that she'd never felt with anyone else. He couldn't have any idea of what the mere act of his sitting beside her did to her. *And to think that I came to the bench to clear my head!* Her mind was more clouded than ever.

He touched her chin with his finger, and she turned, lifting her eyes to meet his. "Emily Cooke." He gave a slight shake of the head. "It's okay. I'll take a step back—or two, or as many as you want. Look, I get it. I'm not looking for anything more than your friendship—not now anyway. Let's give it some time." He leaned closer and lowered his head until he could look up into her eyes, whether she wanted him to or not.

The look on his face was so sincere and vulnerable that it tugged at her heart and weakened her resolve. Her brain was so muddled that it was all she could do not to lean into him and touch her lips to his forehead and cheek and mouth. She took in a breath, hoping the influx of oxygen would do better than her wavering will. "The thing is, I haven't had time to myself for a couple of years. I didn't mind. It was my mom. And my aunt. They were sick. I was all that they had. I would do it all over again." She stopped and fought back the tears that were stinging her eyes. "But it took something out of me—something I came here to find."

"You're grieving, and I know that you need time to work through it. All I'm asking is for some leftover time now and then for us to get to know each other—as friends. No expectations."

She tore her gaze from the horizon and looked into his eyes—eyes that were gentle and sympathetic, which only made her feel worse. "The thing with relationships is, there's no return on investment unless you've got something to give. I've got nothing. My emotions are spent. I just can't. No, that's not it. To be perfectly fair, I just don't want to feel. I don't want you to care. I came here to get away from the people who care. They hovered around me until I just couldn't breathe."

Emily looked away and took a moment to pull herself back together then continued. "I don't want to care whether a pretty woman pulls into your driveway and spends the night. Or why it was worth it for you to spend six months in jail to protect her. I want it—or you—to mean nothing to me."

"I don't blame you for wondering about Vic's visit or my past or anything else. I know how it feels to be desperate for solitude. For six months, I was constantly watched. I was never alone. I came here to escape from that personal hell. When I got here, I could not even stand to make small talk. I had lost faith in humanity. Two people helped drag me out of that dark place. Delia convinced me to work on the lighthouse restoration. And then I met you. But being here and working with you has helped me to see that life isn't all bad. There are good things in life. You've been one of those good things for me, and I think I could be that for you— if you won't shut me out."

"I have to." Emily sighed and looked up. "Even friendship comes with a full set of baggage that neither of us can carry right now."

"You don't have to carry anything, Em. Just let me be here."

"Well, you pretty much are, since you live right next door." Her face wrinkled up into a self-depre-cating smirk. "Sorry. I seem to get stupid when I'm uncomfortable." She let out a nervous sigh. "Which I am. Wes, if I'd met you any other time... I mean, you're pretty good-looking!" She smiled at the understate-ment. "And you're smart and fun. I'm not totally on board with the motorcycle, but I know it's a guy thing. So other than that, you're as close to perfect as they come. But I'm not ready, and it's going to be a long time till I am."

And here come the tears. That just won't do. "Oh, dammit, I can't do this right now." She got up and left for home before her emotions got the better of her. If she cried, it would be on her terms—at home and alone.

TEN

EMILY WALKED into the Anchor Café, where Delia sat waiting for her. "Have you been waiting long?"

"No, not at all."

Emily set her purse down between her feet, an old habit she'd picked up from traveling. "Well, I wanted to have you for lunch, but my cooking is not really up to the task. So I hope you don't mind this. If you tasted my cooking, your palate would thank you."

Delia smiled with her usual warmth. "I'm sure that your cooking is fine. But I always enjoy getting out about town, and having good company makes it even better."

Emily smiled. "Good company might be overstating the case, but I do make an effort."

They were briefly interrupted by a waiter, who

took their order. With that done, Delia said, "So, how is the lighthouse campaign progressing?"

"Well, I think most of my part is done, and Wes has placed all the printing orders and secured some ad space in the local newspapers and a few magazines. So I think everything's where it should be at this point."

Delia gave an approving nod. "This is excellent news. You and Wes make a good team."

Emily leveled a look of caution at her. "I'm sure your teams are doing as well. What else have you got planned?"

Delia moved on as though she had never brought up the topic of Wes. "The fundraising committee has set up a few fundraising events, culminating in a silent auction. One of the local residents made a thermometer sign to track our progress. That's already up on display outside the lighthouse, so we hope to be painting the mercury rising very soon." Delia leaned back and grinned.

"One thing I've learned about you is that you get things done."

"Not everything," Delia said knowingly.

Emily gripped the edge of the table. "Okay. I can see that you won't let this go."

"Only because I care about both of you."

"Delia, I like him. I do. But the timing's not good.

And Wes told me—at your urging, apparently—about the assault and the jail time. He's had his share of troubles, and I've had a difficult few years."

As Delia listened, Emily recapped her time caring for her mom and aunt, filling in any blanks she hadn't already shared. Then she leaned forward. "I didn't mind it one bit, but it was hard to give them what they needed while, at the same time, my work grew more and more demanding. It was my fault. Before I knew how my home life would change, I committed to some conferences and publishing deadlines. And then, for reasons I still don't understand, I got sort of engaged."

Delia squinted with confusion. "Sort of engaged. That sounds like quite a commitment."

"Okay. I got engaged. Maybe I thought it would make my life easier. Or maybe I just wanted a person to lean on—someone who would be there when I had a spare moment."

"I see. So you were deeply in love?" She leaned her chin on her interlaced fingers.

Delia's sarcasm was not lost on Emily. "I know that I sound like a terrible person, but if I was, so was he. I'm not such a practical person by nature, but at that point in my life, I had to be. Oliver was always a practical man, and we worked together, so it was all very convenient. I became good at compartmentalizing my life, but in doing so, I wound up divided into so many pieces, and one of them got lost. That one turned out to be me."

The food arrived. Emily glanced at her salad then lifted her eyes. "I'm so sorry. I've been rambling on."

Delia's eyes softened. "When's the last time anyone listened to you?"

Emily smiled as an ache swelled in her chest. "Actually, you and Wes have been doing a great job of that."

"That's because you deserve it." Delia was quiet for a minute then said, "Have you told Wes any of this?"

"Yes. Well, no. No, I glossed over the part about being engaged—mainly because we broke up right before I came here. I suppose you're going to tell me I owe it to him, but there's no point anymore."

Delia gave Emily the sort of smile her mother might have given her in better days. "I owe you an apology."

Emily leaned back and regarded her with interest. "How so?"

"I know that I've pushed Wes on you, and I'm sorry. You both have the right to make choices without my interference. I'm not usually like this, but I care so much about the two of you. I never had children of my own, and Wes is like a son to me. Anyway..."

Emily moved the bits of salad around with her fork. "To be honest, I look at him, and I think I must be crazy not to be all over him. It's not like he isn't my type. But the two of us are in such wrong places for each other. If only there were a pause button for life. Right now, I'm broken. And Wes doesn't need me in his life."

"Maybe he's a little bit broken himself."

"I know. So the last thing we need is to be broken together. We'd just drag each other down."

Delia glanced up from her sandwich. "Well, I'm sure you won't be surprised to hear that I don't agree, but my new plan is to respect your feelings."

"It was nice of you to try." Emily's face brightened. "Maybe I can return the favor." She glanced about the diner. "I'll keep my eye out for someone who's perfect for you."

Delia's face practically blanched. "You've got a very mean streak in you, young lady."

Emily laughed. "Not really. I just like to give back."

Delia set down the last bite of her sandwich and dabbed her mouth with her napkin. "This might be the perfect time to change the subject." And they did.

EMILY DROVE BACK FROM TOWN, her mind swimming with thoughts of Wes. She appreciated Delia's apology and valued her friendship. Anything she had done had the best of intentions behind it. Emily couldn't remember the last time someone other than family had cared enough to do so much for her. Even as that thought came to her, she realized she'd had friends all around her at work who had wanted to help, and she'd been so lost in a haze of overwhelming responsibility—and eventually grief—that she hadn't been able to reach all those outstretched hands. But she had a friend now, and it meant so much to her.

And then there was Wes. He had offered to give her the time that she needed, and she was inclined to give it to him. Delia adored him, which spoke very highly of Wes. So for now, being friends with him was a good thing.

As she reached that conclusion, she rounded the corner and noticed a car in her driveway. It wasn't just any car. It belonged to Oliver Whitehead, her sort-of fiancé. Her gut feeling and her common sense both told her to run. She wished she could drive past her house and keep going. But Oliver didn't miss a thing, so she knew he'd spot her car. She wouldn't even have put it past him to make chase in his own vehicle. So she braced herself and pulled into the driveway. He got out of his car and waited by the front steps. At the moment, he looked like some sort of guard dog making sure she would not get away. She hid her unpleasant surprise with a pasted-on smile as he sauntered toward her.

"Emmy!" He smiled confidently, pulled her into his arms, and kissed her.

"Oliver?" She could almost feel the furrows deepening on her forehead, but she couldn't help it. "What brings you here? Is something the matter?"

"Yes, in a way." He lifted his shoulders and nodded.

Now she was alarmed. "Is your family okay?"

He looked surprised. "Yeah, they're fine."

Well, that was a relief. She had spent time with them when they visited Oliver, and she'd enjoyed every visit.

"I took a couple of days off so I could come see you."

"But... I wasn't expecting you."

"Yeah, I know, the break. But a funeral is no place to make life-changing decisions, so I thought you might have reconsidered." He shrugged bashfully. "I've missed you. We need to talk."

What he meant was that he needed to talk. The last thing she needed or wanted was a talk with Oliver.

All she wanted was the same thing she'd wanted from the day she'd arrived—time alone to figure out what came next.

Oliver gazed into her eyes. "You've changed."

She didn't know what to say to that. If she had changed, it had been for the better. Maybe his visit would make that clear. Seeing Oliver brought back all her memories of how they used to be. Maybe his being here would bring their relationship into focus without the distractions they'd dealt with before.

"So, how long are you here for?" she asked.

"Just a couple of days."

Then she heard a familiar rumble of an approaching motorcycle. She hooked her arm about Oliver's. "Oh my gosh, look at my manners. Let's go inside and talk." She pulled his arm, but he resisted.

"I'll just grab my bag from the car."

"Oh, we can do that later."

He freed himself from her grasp and headed straight for the car, which was parked in her driveway. Wes rode into his driveway, only yards from where Oliver had parked. He got off of his bike and pulled off his helmet, making no effort to hide the fact that he was looking their way. Emily stared back while Oliver, oblivious to them, pulled out his suitcase and turned as he closed the door behind him. At that point, time had nearly slowed to a stop as Emily watched the whole awkward event unfold. Oliver waved and called out a hello, no doubt because he saw Wes staring at them. Wes returned the wave, his eyes darting toward Emily as he started to walk over the grassy divide between the two driveways. Her jaw hung open as she watched them shake hands and exchange introductions. The scene was a blur that ended with Oliver calling her name.

As she headed toward the two men, Emily sized up the flowerpots lining the steps of her porch, just in case she needed a place to get sick on her way back inside. There was no salvaging anything now.

"Hi, Em."

"Wes." *Great.* She glanced at Oliver. His face barely registered a reaction, but she knew him. He was taking it all in. A nickname added a layer to a relationship, which in turn added a layer to the tension already between her and Oliver. "I see you've met Oliver."

Wes nodded and turned to Oliver. "So you are Emily's, uh..."

Oliver nodded. "Fiancé."

"Sort of!" she hastened to add.

Wes then launched into autopilot with the typical questions locals the world over ask of their visitors. "So, is this your first time to Cape Cod?"

"Yes, it is."

"And what do you think?"

"I love it."

"I hope you like seafood." Not once did Wes look at Emily.

"Oh, well, I have a shellfish allergy."

"That's a shame."

Please, God, make it end soon.

Wes scratched his head and looked off into the distance. "How was your drive?"

"Like driving into a funnel." They laughed, and Oliver launched into a mind-numbing rhapsody on driving in America and the good time he'd managed to have. Wes listened amiably, never once glancing Emily's way. At one point, she thought she saw the corner of his mouth twitch just a little, but she couldn't be sure.

"Yeah, only had to stop once."

"Well, we'd better let you go." She hadn't meant to cut Oliver off so vigorously, but one way or the other, it had to be done. She smiled sweetly to Wes, which elicited a sparkle in his eye. She averted her eyes and grasped hold of Oliver's arm. "Bye." She came just short of dragging him back to her house.

Once inside, Oliver said, "That was a little abrupt."

"Oh, was it?" She did her best imitation of nonchalance then quickly changed the subject. "So, Oliver, why are you here?"

"Why, yes, *Em*. I'd love a glass of water."

Without saying a word, she went into the kitchen and got it for him. There was no use trying to guide the conversation. As usual, Oliver would do what he wanted when he wanted. If she seemed too eager to know something—like why he was there—he would take even longer to tell her. It was just one of his little control-freak idiosyncrasies that she'd trained herself to ignore.

She sat down in the second most comfortable chair. Oliver had already helped himself to the first, which was fine. He was her guest, albeit an uninvited one.

With no warning, Oliver launched into his speech, which she had no doubt he'd prepared in advance. That was another thing about him she had learned to tolerate, which reminded her of yet another: it was best not to interrupt him during one of his speeches, because he would back up and retrace his thoughts.

"The truth is, I've missed you. I know that we talked about taking a break."

"Well... not quite a break. Breaking up." But as she said it, she remembered she had never returned the ring, so it wasn't official.

His eyebrows drew together. "I specifically recall our discussing a break."

Emily looked up and recalled. "That's what you wanted, so I agreed for the time being." *So I wouldn't have to argue with you.*

He nodded with that triumphant smile of his. "The plan was that you would come here, and I would stay there."

"Yet here you are."

"You don't have to be petty."

Emily nodded. "You're right."

Oliver opened his mouth, but Emily went on. "Whatever sort of break it is, you initiated it because I wasn't giving you enough attention—when my mother was dying."

"Now, hold on there."

"No. You were right." But her tone shifted. "Everything that you said makes so much sense to me now. Taking a break was the best thing to do. And it's gone so well that I think we should make it permanent. Hold on—I'll go get the ring."

He reached out and grasped her wrist. His voice softened. "Emily, you can't make a decision tonight. I just got here. Let's sleep on it."

She hoped he understood that their sleeping on it would not happen together. Just to be clear, she said, "Excuse me while I get some bedding for the sofa."

Oliver stood and drew closer. "You wouldn't make me sleep on the sofa. You know how my back is."

"I'll bring in the chaise lounge cushion from the porch. We can stretch it out on the floor, nice and flat." She walked away, marveling at the signature Oliver Whitehead temerity. It made her feel so much less guilty.

She'd give him his ring in the morning.

ELEVEN

Emily spent the night tossing and turning, so at the first sign of daylight, she was out of the house, leaving Oliver snoring behind her. There was no use in looking for anything positive in his actions. Oliver was all about pleasing Oliver. What she needed to do was to clear her own head, so she left the engagement ring on her dresser and went for a run.

It wasn't as if she'd never had feelings for the man. In fact, the problem was that she had. Apparently, there was no accounting for taste—even hers. So many times, she had longed for a word or a gesture that might convey genuine feeling for her. In that sense, she'd known there was something missing almost from the start. But they had so much in common—their work and... well, work was a huge common interest. After all, how much time did one spend at work? So it only made sense that they'd wind up together. She frowned to herself. Actually, it made no sense that they'd wound up together. They had nothing in common but work and convenience. If work was the foundation of their relationship, convenience was the glue that bound them together, whether both of them liked it or not. In a way, it hadn't been so bad. There were times when it was nice to have a companion to go with her to faculty events and professorial dinners or just to fill in the odd Saturday night so they wouldn't be alone.

And now here he was, which on its own was a surprise. More surprising than that was the fact that she felt nothing for him—at all. Except that she wanted him gone. She had to find some way to say it so it wouldn't hurt his feelings. Although she didn't know why she should worry about his feelings when he'd never given hers a thought. How many times had she begged off a date or a social engagement because her mother or aunt was too ill to be left alone? Oliver would moan and complain about how she was ruining his career or his evening or how she just wasn't fun. After a while, his grumbling became like white noise or a leaky faucet. She knew it was there, but she didn't interact with it.

But her sense of self-worth—or maybe simply her good sense—had been awakened. Apparently, having time on her own was all she had needed to reach that point. She was rested and clearheaded. But her new sense of self-worth was mainly because of Wes. With all of their false starts and bad timing—even though they weren't even a thing—he still made her feel better, more cared for, than her own fiancé. That was something to ponder.

Before any pondering could happen, her foot caught on some driftwood, and she did a face-plant in the dirt path leading up to the lighthouse. She lay still, afraid to move for fear that she had injured herself so much that she would fall apart. Did her neck need to be stabilized? *Wow, I really need to ease up on the firefighter TV shows.*

She was pulled from her dazed state of mind by the repetitive buzzing of her phone, which had flown from her pocket and landed just beyond reach. Stretching farther awakened a new world of pain. She collapsed then gathered the strength to make one more try. This time she grasped it. She groaned when she saw that the screen, while still intact—thanks to her screen protector—had shattered from the corner and spread in a spiderweb pattern to the opposite end of the phone.

"Oh, crap. Because I got a new phone last month. If I'd kept the old phone, I would never have fallen."

A text message appeared, giving her hope that her phone still worked. It read, "Was that you?"

The message was from Wes. She tried to reply, but

the phone refused to respond to her touch. After an exasperated sound and a few more attempts, she gave up. It was useless.

Well, I can't stay here all day. I'd better try to get up and go home. She pulled herself up to a sitting position. She was feeling a little bit better except for the shaking, no doubt due to the surplus of adrenaline coursing through her system. Having made that much progress, she decided to stand. And then sit. That wasn't good. Her ankle refused to support her full weight. She couldn't blame it, really. It was quite a burden to bear. And yet her ankle had been doing just fine until that moment.

"Em!"

She turned around to find Wes rushing toward her. He knelt by her side. "What happened? Where does it hurt?"

"I fell, and I've messed up my ankle."

"Okay. My car's over there in the lot."

"You drove over here?"

He wrinkled his face. "It's a one-minute drive, and I thought you might not be up for a long walk on the beach."

"Good call. But how did you know that I'd fallen?"

"Relax. I'm not stalking you."

"I didn't say you were. I was just thinking what a Boy Scout you are. So you saw me fall and drove over?"

"I was just sitting outside, having my morning coffee, when I looked over and saw someone take a tumble on their way up the embankment to the lighthouse."

"I wouldn't call it a tumble exactly. It was more of a trip."

"You didn't answer my text."

"The force of me falling on it was too much for my phone."

He half smiled and lifted his eyes from her ankle, which had occupied his examining hands and attention for the last minute or so. "Can you move it?"

"Not without swearing like a sailor. At you."

"I think we'd better get you to the hospital."

Emily wanted to disagree, but she couldn't stand up or walk. She had to concede that something was wrong, and that something probably required a doctor's attention.

With no warning, Wes began barking orders—or at least, that was how it sounded to her. But everything was filtered through pain. She wanted to send him away and take care of herself, but she had to admit that she couldn't. At the moment, he was her only option. As frustrated as she was becoming, she had to defer to the adage that beggars could not be choosers. So she took hold of his hooked forearm and allowed him to pull her to her feet—or rather, foot, since one ankle was clearly out of commission. As instructed, Emily put her arm around Wes's neck then hopped alongside him all the way back to his car. Even through the pain, she could not help but notice how good it felt to be—sort of—in his arms. She landed in the passenger seat with a sigh, then she carefully lifted her leg and even more carefully set it back down on the floorboard.

Wes leaned on the doorframe and looked down with concern. "Are you sure you wouldn't rather sit in the back seat and stretch your leg out?"

She leaned back against the headrest and helplessly lifted her eyes. "Would it require moving?"

He winced. "Bad idea?"

"No, the back seat was a good idea, but the moving part wasn't."

"Okay, then. Let's go. Watch your fingers."

As he closed the door, she muttered to herself, "I'm not five."

He hopped into the driver's seat and backed out of the parking lot. "So I thought you were more of a walker. What possessed you to run?"

"I needed some air. So I thought, what with all the gasping, I'd get some."

"Good. For a minute, I thought you might have been running from something."

She answered him with a sharp sideways look, then

she leaned back, closed her eyes, and pulled the bill of her baseball cap down to her nose.

"Tired?" He lifted an eyebrow and added, "For some reason?"

Emily sat up abruptly then moaned from the pain.

"Easy there."

Emily exhaled loudly. "Are you trying to annoy me, or do you just have a gift?"

The only hint of a reaction was the slight upturn of his mouth at the edge, which she chose to ignore. He hadn't meant mere lack of sleep. He was needling her. She felt as though each remark was designed to annoy her, make fun of Oliver and his sudden appearance, or draw information from her—maybe all of the above. Or she might just be overreacting. He had, after all, come running to her rescue, which was a pretty nice thing to do. If she'd waited for Oliver, gangrene would have set in—not to mention winter. But her body would be well preserved for the spring.

"Oh, Oliver!"

"No, Wes. Oliver's the other man in your life."

"The other man? Oh, never mind. I just remembered, he doesn't know where I am. He'll be worried."

Wes cast a wry look at her. "Yeah, he strikes me as the worrying kind."

"You don't know him!" she said, although, from the sound of it, he had Oliver pretty well sized up. "Never mind. I've got to call him." She patted her hips until she found her phone in the back zipper pocket of her running shorts. "Oh, crap. I forgot and sat on it."

"Am I going to have to pull shards of glass from your—"

"No!" She muttered, "It's not broken like that. The screen protector is holding it together." She pressed and swiped at her phone for a bit then tossed it into the recessed compartment of Wes's dashboard.

Wes kept glancing over. "Is it broken?"

"Yeah. Your text was its last hurrah."

Wes held out his phone. "Here. Use mine."

She took it and stared for a moment then handed it back. "I can't. I don't know his number."

"He's your sort-of fiancé, and you don't know his number?"

"I didn't have to. It was saved in my phone."

Wes handed the phone back. "Then just call your house number."

Her frustration faded. "Oh, right." She held the phone, poised to dial. "Wes?"

"Yeah?"

"Do you know my phone number?"

He glanced at her then stared at the road. From the look on his face, he would have shut his eyes if he hadn't been driving. Emily let her hand drop to her lap. She could tell he was suppressing a laugh. She deserved it, but still, he didn't need to make his amusement so obvious.

He put his hand over hers. "Relax, Em. We'll figure it out."

THE TWO OF them sat in the emergency room with Emily's leg stretched out over Wes's lap. Emily grasped his shoulder. "Whatever you do, please don't move."

"Promise." He gave her a reassuring nod and resumed studying her ankle. "It's swollen."

"How do you know? Maybe I've got chronic cankles."

Wes's eyes crinkled with amusement. "I may have stolen a glance once or twice—to establish a baseline."

Her eyebrows furrowed with an indignation she couldn't quite maintain.

Wes peered into her eyes. "It was purely academic curiosity."

Emily was secretly pleased he had noticed her ankles. But that made her vexed with herself. She had too many mixed feelings to sort through. "Academic?"

"My study of your ankles." A boyish grin bloomed on his face. As if that weren't bad enough, she grinned with him.

"Emily!"

"Oliver?"

In he rushed then stopped and took in the sight of Emily's leg resting comfortably on Wes's lap and the two of them unabashedly grinning at one another.

She eyed Oliver with wonder. "How did you find me?"

Wes said, "I called him. When I got up a while ago."

"Ms. Cooke?" A nurse stood waiting and glancing about the waiting room.

Emily stood up and started to hop, but the nurse said, "Sit back down. I'll go get you a wheelchair."

Emily sat and turned to Wes. "But how did you get the number?"

"I called Delia. Turns out she knows your house number since she owns the place."

"Thanks, Wes." Oliver smiled and put his arm around Emily's shoulder.

The nurse returned and helped Emily into a wheelchair and wheeled her away. Emily stole a quick glance at the two men who sat together waiting for her. *There ought to be good times ahead there.* She shuddered as she refused to imagine what they'd manage to talk about.

An hour later, a nurse wheeled Emily out of an examining room wearing an orthopedic boot for what turned out to be a sprained ankle.

Wes and Oliver stood up in tandem.

Emily met Wes's eyes. "Thank you."

Oliver chimed in. "I told him he didn't have to wait."

Wes looked almost bashful. "I wanted to make sure you were okay. It looks like you are, so I'll be on my way."

Wait! Don't leave me! She practically blurted it out but caught herself just in time. "Thanks for everything, Wes."

He flashed the winning smile that always made her knees buckle. Luckily, she was in a wheelchair. The nurse must have taken one look at Wes and known she would need it. Wes almost seemed to know how that particular expression affected the ladies—this lady—and smiled on purpose just to taunt her. *No, that's crazy talk.* She was reading way too much into the whole thing. He was just being nice.

"Emily?"

She turned toward Oliver with a blank expression. "Hmm?"

"I'll go get the car." As Oliver walked to his car, Wes drove past and gave a quick wave.

She'd almost forgotten the nurse standing behind

her wheelchair until she heard her voice. "Looks like you'll have plenty of help while you recover."

"Oh, yes. Plenty."

Oliver pulled up and hopped out of the car. "Are you okay to walk on that thing?"

"Uh, maybe."

The nurse put the brakes on the wheelchair and lifted the footrests. With the combined efforts of the nurse and Oliver, she managed to get out of the chair and into the car. As she thanked the nurse and they pulled away from the entrance, Emily looked at Oliver and realized the best part of her day was behind her.

TWELVE

THE LATE-AFTERNOON SUN hung in the sky as if waiting for Emily to hobble out to her porch with a beer. And as she walked out and arranged herself in a chair with her foot propped up, a gentle rain began to patter upon the tin roof that covered the porch. It had waited for her. She didn't mind it. In fact, she enjoyed the gentle sound and the smell of fresh rain and the sea. And being alone. Oliver was gone.

Wes appeared at the side of the porch. "Hey, I saw you over here all alone, and I thought I'd drop off some of my medicinal brew." He rounded the porch and arrived at the steps. "Shall I put these in the fridge?"

"Are you kidding? That's too far to walk. Sit down. We'll just have to drink fast while they're still cold."

Wes looked down uncomfortably. "Oh, I think Oliver's seen enough of me for one day."

"And me too. He's gone." She waved her arm toward the chair beside her, and he sat.

Wes took a swig of his beer. "Gone... for good?"

As she nodded, she thought she saw his eyes brighten a bit. She took way too much pleasure in the mere possibility of it. "Gone with a ring in his pocket."

"Oh, wow." He looked suddenly somber. "I'm sorry."

"I don't want to talk about it. But I'll drink to it." She lifted her beer and clinked it against his.

They sat for a while in comfortable quiet with only the sound of the rain to intrude on the moment. Emily set down her beer and pulled one from Wes's six-pack. She tried to twist the cap off, but he shook his head and held out his hand. "Allow me." He pulled out a pocket-sized bottle opener.

"Wow, you are a Boy Scout."

He handed the bottle to her. "Yeah, their motto is *Be prepared*. Although I don't think they had a beer bottle opener in mind."

Emily smiled. "Maybe not, but in this case, I'm not complaining."

She leaned back and turned her head toward Wes. "I don't think I've thanked you enough. If you hadn't come looking for me—"

"Someone would have happened along when the

lighthouse opened to visitors. But I'm glad I could help."

She was sure she could feel the warmth in his gaze, but when he kept looking into her eyes, she knew she was in trouble. His lips parted as if he were going to say something. From his expression, it was something she wanted to hear, but he turned and took a drink of his beer.

Then his demeanor changed, and he said, "You don't mind being alone, do you?"

"No, I don't. Sometimes I prefer it."

"I hope now isn't one of those times."

Is he actually worried? "No." She smiled to herself while she decided whether to say it. "I actually don't hate being with you."

He lifted his beer in a toast. "Another shining endorsement from the ladies!"

She couldn't help but laugh. "No, really. I like being with you." How had he gotten that confession from her?

He looked straight at her with a guileless expression. "I like being with you, too, Emily Cooke." Just as she was marveling at how a simple statement could give her such a thrill, he said, "I don't miss Oliver, though. But I'm just being selfish." His smile faded, and his gaze drifted away as he reached over and put his hand on hers. As he laced their fingers together, he stared out at the beach, where the sand was now darkened and dimpled by rain. "This is the best time I've had in a long time."

"You need to get out more." She turned and smiled, but his soft, searching eyes disarmed any defenses she had left. "Me too." In that moment, something shifted between them. She looked down, overwhelmed. "To be honest, my life hasn't exactly been full of good times lately."

Wes turned toward her and leaned on his elbow, a move that required letting go of her hand. She supposed they couldn't have gone on living with hands locked together, but still, she missed his touch the minute it was gone.

He said, "You've mentioned your mother. That must have been hard."

She nodded and tamped down a sudden swell of emotion. "It was. In a strange way, I felt closer to her than I'd ever been before—to my aunt too. Both were diabetics—the family-DNA curse. It was almost like clockwork the way my mother died months after my aunt, following the same pattern, the same awful progression. But through their suffering, they seized life. On good days, there was laughter and joy, and on bad ones, well... I guess they just soldiered on."

"You soldiered on." His frank gaze pierced her

veneer. She'd never felt so honest or so emotionally raw.

"You do what you have to." She stared out to the stormy gray sea then smiled as a memory came to her.

"What?" He peered curiously at her.

This was far down the list of things she would have chosen to share. Maybe his coming to her rescue had made her trust him. She felt comfortable with him in a way she hadn't before. "Okay. It's an Oliver story."

Wes's eyes narrowed, but he continued to listen.

"One night, my aunt wasn't feeling too well, and my mother wasn't much better. So I cancelled a date. Well, it wasn't just a date. It was dinner at the dean's house, and Oliver was campaigning heavily for a promotion. So it wasn't like I was just missing dinner and drinks. Still, my family needed me, and Oliver didn't. Although that wasn't his version."

Wes wrinkled his face in disbelief.

"According to him, I was ruining his life if not his career. Looking back, that was the beginning of the end. But I actually felt oddly relieved. I hung up the phone, made some popcorn, and the three of us spent the evening binge-watching costume dramas. It was so peaceful and pleasant—everything Oliver wasn't."

"And when was that?"

"Over a year ago."

"If you felt that way back then, what kept you with him so long?"

"Slow learner, I guess," she said.

"Never mind. I'm prying."

She looked straight at him. "I've been asking myself that for months. I still don't quite know the answer. It started because we seemed to have so much in common. From the outside. But we were just two different people on parallel paths. We continued to go through the motions because we'd begun."

"I can't say I've ever done that in a relationship, but I have in a job. Sometimes you just hang on because you get so bogged down in the details of each busy day that you forget what the outside world looks like."

Emily nodded and stared off into the distance. "One day, my mother was sick—more than usual—so I broke a date, and Oliver broke off the relationship. He was sick and tired of having to adjust to my life—to my mother's whims, as he put it. He called it 'taking a break.' I guess that was his way of softening the blow. And I was too lazy to have the discussion we really needed to have, so I left it at that. The next day, she died. I went through the arrangements and funeral alone. Everyone I had loved was now gone. And there I was, standing in the shadows of life. I was lost. I didn't even know who I was anymore. So I took a sabbatical leave."

He looked wholly contented gazing at her. "And now you're here."

"It was just what I needed—that and gas for my car."

Wes grinned.

"And then yesterday, I'd just come from having lunch with Delia. I was thinking about how good it felt to have friends. Then Oliver showed up."

"With no warning?"

"Nope. Just showed up on my doorstep. Yay!" Her grin shifted to a smirk. "He didn't even want me, not really. He loved what he thought he could shape me into. I guess I mistook that for him loving me. But when we got home from the hospital, he started to complain that I should have been more careful. What was I thinking? That injury was really gonna put a damper on his visit. Then I had this sudden road-to-Damascus moment. Right then and there, I decided I wasn't going to Damascus. But he could, for all I cared. I just wanted him gone. So I gave back the ring."

"That can't have been easy." If it was possible to look both sympathetic and secretly happy, Wes did.

Emily thought for a moment. "I didn't want to hurt him, so I tried to let him down gently. But it was so long overdue that I didn't even feel guilty about it. I'd given so much of myself that his loss didn't come close in comparison."

Wes leaned forward. "Well, that's just not true."

Lost in her own thoughts of the breakup, Emily looked at him, confused.

"Losing you was the worst thing that will ever happen to him."

"So now you're a fortuneteller?"

He reached out and took hold of her hand. "I don't need to be a fortuneteller to know how amazing you are."

Never one to accept a compliment well, Emily smirked. "Maybe you just have low standards."

He gave her a stern look, then he stood and tugged at her hand. "Come here. I want to show you something."

She couldn't guess what it could be, but she stood as he'd requested.

"Oh. Your ankle. Are you okay to stand?"

"For a minute or two."

He stood facing her and took hold of both of her hands. "I'm planning to show you just how wrong you are, and those chairs just weren't going to work. I should warn you. This might involve kissing. So if that's not what you want, tell me now, because I am so lost in you that once I start, I might not want to stop."

"Well, okay, but I don't understand wh—" Before she'd finished the last word, his lips were on hers, and he proved true to his word. He kissed her until she tightened her grip on his shoulders to steady her balance. "I'd better sit down."

"It's getting dark out here. Why don't we go in?"

"Wes, I'm not ready to jump into—"

"Bed? That's okay."

She wrinkled her eyebrows. "I was going to say another relationship, but okay, bed too."

He winced. "Ouch. That was smooth."

Emily couldn't help but grin. "That's okay."

"My point, at least now, is this: take as much time as you need. I'm not going anywhere—unless you want me to."

"No, I don't want that."

"Good." He kissed her again. Then he tore himself away with an agonized sigh, led her by the hand to the living room sofa, and picked up the TV remote.

THE PREVIOUS NIGHT'S rain had cleared the air, and the morning sun shone on what promised to be a magnificent day. But then, Emily's outlook had changed. Any day would have looked promising. Wes had picked her up for an outing. They sat in his car under an open sunroof and a soothing, warm breeze.

Emily glanced over at Wes, who had one of those

faces just made for sunglasses. "So what's on the agenda?"

"Us."

"Us?" That wasn't exactly an answer.

"Isn't that enough for you? It's all I need for today."

"You're being deliberately vague."

"Well, the truth is, I wasn't quite sure what we could do with your ankle out of commission. Bicycling was out, and I thought of a picnic, but I doubt you can manage a sandy beach in that boot."

"No," she said. "I'm not really much fun with this thing."

"Now, I didn't say that. I just want to do something that won't cause you excruciating pain—'cause I'm thoughtful like that."

"Yes, you are."

"So, you seem to do okay sitting."

"Like a boss."

"Good," he said. "So how 'bout whale watching?"

"I would love to!"

In no time, they were on the deck of the next whale-watching boat heading out to sea. Emily lifted her face to the wind as Wes put an arm around her shoulder. They'd secured spots on the first row of benches, a perfect vantage point. She would have been happy to sit there all morning, whales or not. But as the thought came to her, a whale shot into the air and flipped over.

As people rushed to the side of the boat, blocking the view, Emily turned to Wes. "Sorry. It's not quite as much fun with a booted companion."

He leaned closer. "Oh, I've already thought of a way to compensate." He kissed her, and his eyes twinkled. "You're much more fun than a whale."

She opened her mouth to say something then settled for a puzzled squint. "Thank you?" With a small fist pump, she said, "Personal goal achieved."

He laughed and drew her close. "That might not have come out like I meant it."

She shook her head, nuzzled against him. "I'm just worried that I've peaked now and may never attain such heights again."

He clutched her against him. "I have faith in you, Em."

THIRTEEN

A LATE FOG rolled in as Wes and Emily sat at a window-side table at Letty's Lobster Shanty. The server set down two steaming cups of clam chowder. Emily took one spoonful and sighed. After a few hours at sea in the wind, it was good to be inside, warmed by hot chowder. She felt completely relaxed and halfway in love.

"Penny for your thoughts."

Well, if that isn't uncanny timing. His blue eyes bored through her and caught her off guard, but she gathered her wits. "I was thinking of how good it feels to be inside and warm and..."

"And...?"

A tinge of guilt crept into her as she smiled. "And with... tolerable company."

He put his hand on hers and ran his thumb over

her palm. He would have to stop doing that, or she'd lose her resolve to move slowly. In fact, at the moment, she wanted to crawl over the table—clam chowder be damned—and see where things might go from there.

"Tolerable, am I? That's high praise, indeed. And you are the most tolerable woman I've spent time with in a long while." He peered into her eyes with so knowing a gaze that no words were needed. They both felt it, but saying it aloud might topple the delicate balance of emotions, not to mention restraint. So they just smiled and left it at that.

Later on, as they lingered over their Chilean chardonnay, Wes turned from the window he'd been staring through. "Tomorrow, I'm going to court."

"Oh?" What was there to say? He'd introduced the subject with no warning. She wasn't prepared.

"Weeks ago, I was served with some papers. You already know I spent six months in jail. Well, that was a criminal case. This is a civil case for the same incident as before. My old boss is suing me. I'm telling you now because I want you to know the truth. I'm sure the story will wind up in the papers. If this is anything like the last time, some of it will be true, and more of it won't. I want you to hear it from me. There's no way you can know that my version is the truth. I can only tell you it is."

Emily looked through the window at the boats

docked in the harbor. "Trust is a strange thing. To be honest, it doesn't come easily to me. Delia has great faith in you. That has helped me to arrive at this point." Turning back to him, she was touched by the uncertainty in his eyes.

"And where's that?"

"Maybe I'm like those fishermen. Day after day, they get into their boats, and they go out to sea with no assurance that the weather won't turn against them or their boats won't break down. But they go out to sea anyway. They do it because they want to or need to. For me, maybe it's both. I want to trust you, and I'm finding I need to."

He tightened his grasp of her hand.

"But don't misunderstand me," she said, growing more serious. "I don't want or need anything enough to suffer a lie. One lie, and it's over."

"Fair enough. Based on what came out in the criminal trial, I have every reason to expect that you'll hear and read lies in the coming days. I can't control any of that. But I stand by the things that I've told you. I did what I felt was the right thing to do. And I'd do it again."

Emily leaned back in her chair. "Maybe that's where we need to begin. Would you tell me about it?"

EMILY HANDED WES one of the beers she'd brought out to the porch. He'd suggested they go back home to talk, which meant he expected emotions to get out of control. Regardless of which end of the spectrum their emotions wound up on, outside seemed the best place to be. Being out on the porch left her with a place to escape to, one less conducive to temptation. She wasn't so worried about Wes as about her own weakness.

Wes sat on the porch rail. "So, here's the short version. If you'd like any details, I can fill you in later. However, after you've heard the short version, it may be enough."

Emily leaned against one of the porch pillars and took a sip of her beer, bracing herself.

"Elliot Lewis was my boss. He was also a horrible person. Everyone knew it. But he was a powerful man in the industry—still is. So it was just overlooked. Lewis hired two types of women: stunningly beautiful and brilliant—and preferably both, although hardly ever just the latter. He hired men too. Somebody needed to play rounds of golf and sit in the skyboxes at games. Not that women couldn't play sports. He just didn't want to play with them. Maybe he was afraid they would beat him.

"He'd been harassing women for years. So by the time I was hired, there was an office-whisper network. Of course, it was months before anyone told me about it. I couldn't blame them. Why trust me, when Lewis had hired me? For all they knew, I was just a younger version of him. And then I nearly walked into the copy room, where Lewis had a female new hire cornered. I stepped back and thought fast. From the hallway, I called her name and walked in with an, 'Oh, there you are!' Someone else in a nearby cube saw what I'd done, and she inducted me into the network."

Emily listened intently.

"It was impressive, really, how well organized it had become. When a new hire came onboard, one of the women would take her under her wing and let her know in vague terms that if she ever needed to talk about anything, she could come to her. The situation was tricky, because they couldn't come out and acknowledge the problem openly—that is, if they wanted to keep their jobs. We never knew whom we could trust. He had his network of spies. Anyway, his typical pattern was to target one woman for a period of time—usually weeks, sometimes months. When Vic—Victoria—joined us, she learned pretty quickly how it was. He seemed to especially like her. I sometimes wonder if it wasn't her kindness that attracted him. It was like a challenge to him—to destroy her inherent goodness. Whatever it was, he went after her with a doggedness that would have been admirable if directed toward any other purpose. But he was a vile animal who would not be dissuaded.

"One day, he called her into his office. By that time, it had become such a common occurrence that the well-oiled machine immediately kicked into gear. We took turns so it wouldn't be obvious what we were doing. A woman with a cube near his office kept track of the rotation and texted the next one in line, using private cell phones so as not to leave a trail of bread crumbs on the office network. Whoever came up in the rotation would spring into action and rescue the current person of interest with a random excuse."

Emily took Wes's empty bottle and went to the kitchen. As she returned with an ice-cold replacement, she said, "It's so impressive, the way that they coped."

Wes gave a nod. "I thought so, too, at first. But looking back, we behaved like downtrodden prisoners who were too fearful to stand up and cry out against something we knew was wrong."

Emily shook her head. "It's easy to talk about taking a stand—unless you're in the middle of it. There are so many factors that cloud a situation. Money, for one. Or career goals. Or just needing a job you can count on to support your family."

Wes shrugged. "It was such a prestigious place to work—one more step toward that lifelong career goal. All they had to do was endure the indignity of it." He frowned. "It sounds bad, but more than one woman told me that."

Emily exhaled and looked away. "It's not always as easy as one might think to be noble, especially when it could ruin your career for the rest of your life. That's a very long time."

Wes lifted an eyebrow. "Yes, I'm fully aware."

Emily winced.

"Anyway, on this particular day, Lewis's secretary heard sounds from inside the office. She couldn't understand the exact words, but Vic raised her voice, and the door handle was rattled. Lewis's secretary signaled the secret office dispatcher to text the next one in the queue, which was me. I was going to barge in with apologies and tell Vic her doctor's office was on hold and had said it was urgent. But this time, the door was locked. Lewis barked, 'Not now.' I turned to his secretary and softly asked for a key, but she shook her head. She didn't have one.

"Vic cried out. I could hear noises—something or someone bumping against the wall. I tried to force open the door, but I couldn't. It was too heavy. So I grabbed a fire extinguisher and slammed it down on the knob until it broke. I barged in. He was on top of her on the sofa. She was fighting him off, but his full weight was on her. I grabbed his shoulders and yanked him away then threw him to the floor. Then I saw that his pants were unzipped, and I punched him in the face.

"By then, Vic had straightened her clothes and her hair and fled Lewis's office. I later was told that she grabbed her valise and went home. Minutes later, the police arrived and arrested me for assault. If they bought my side of the story, they didn't show it. But that didn't surprise me. Lewis knew too many people in Boston. He knew where the bodies were buried, so he bought his way out of trouble—and bought my way into it. Denied bail, I spent six months in jail during the trial and was eventually sentenced to time served."

"And then you came here."

"To escape pretty much everyone. I lost faith in humanity. That hasn't changed much, actually."

Emily touched his hand. "It's no wonder after what you've been through."

"So now round two begins. I guess I should have expected it. Ruining my career wasn't enough. Elliot must've gotten hold of my financial information—enough to know I'm a trust-fund beneficiary. It's not as though he needs the money. He just doesn't want me to have it. Or maybe he just wants the delight of watching me lose it."

Quietly, Emily said, "You did the right thing."

He looked into her eyes with a mixture of appreciation and sorrow. "I know. And I'd do it again. Which is not to say that it's easy."

She gave his hand a squeeze. "The right thing so often is like that."

"I wonder, though, how much good it did, really. Lewis is still there—up to his same old tricks. So what good did I do?"

Emily said, "If you don't know the answer to that—and I think you do—you could always ask Vic."

Wes looked into her eyes. "So this is who you've gotten yourself involved with."

Emily tore her gaze from Wes's eyes before she poured out everything that was in her heart. "I'm sorry for not believing in you. If you'd only have told me..."

"You didn't know me well enough. Don't you think I could see how things changed after you read about me in the paper?"

"Because I didn't understand."

"No. I decided before I met you that I was done trying to explain."

It hurt her to think that he viewed her as just another person who would never trust him. "It would've been nice if you had given me a chance."

Wes met her frustration with an emotionless stare. "I gave you what you deserved—to not get involved in my mess of a life. You can't say I didn't try to spare you."

She was tired of keeping her distance while the two of them danced around one another like a pair of punch-drunk boxers. "Did I ask to be spared?"

"It was written all over your face, everything that you said—and didn't say. I knew all the signs because I was here doing the same thing. Escaping. Picking up the pieces of my life—of myself."

She wanted to protest but couldn't, because he was right.

Wes reached over and brushed his fingers over her hand. "Em, I was just so damned weary. I got to a point where I just didn't care what anyone thought. All I wanted was to be left alone."

"I would've understood."

He lowered his chin and fixed doubtful eyes on her, putting her on the defensive. "Maybe not at first, but with Delia to vouch for you, I would've come around. But you just wouldn't bother."

"It wasn't because you weren't worth it. It's because you were. The risk of pain was too much. I couldn't do it."

"So you decided," he said.

"People decide every day. They go on a dating app and swipe left or right. They go out on that second date, or they don't. No one has to explain—and very few do. Sometimes it's better that way." Emily folded her arms. "It's not fair."

"Welcome to my world. There's no such thing as fair."

"That's a cynical way to live life."

Wes shrugged. "No argument here. But life does that to people."

Emily couldn't decide whether to feel angry at or sorry for Wes.

He took her hand in his and gazed into her eyes. "But then, life does things that take you by surprise. Just when I'd gotten used to my new way of life as a bitter recluse, this woman showed up who had run out of gas. And I found myself wanting to know her."

His mouth slowly spread into a smile, banishing all thoughts of frustration and anger she'd felt moments before. Fearing her face would broadcast the entire contents of her heart before she was quite ready, she averted her eyes.

He touched his fingertips to her chin and turned her around to face him. "I still want to know you. More each day." Then he kissed her, and she lost control of her emotions. The way his kiss made her head spin was nothing compared to what was going on in her heart. She could no longer lie to herself. She was falling in love, and she hoped that she wasn't alone.

Wes took an exaggerated step backward and shook his head. "Emily Cooke. If I didn't have court tomorrow, I'd be saying something different right now." His penetrating stare made her pulse quicken.

She put her arms about his neck and breathed in his scent. It was all she could do not to bodily drag him into her bedroom—not that she physically could have. *But if he keeps looking at me like that, I'll try, damn it.*

He slid his hands down her arms and took hold of hers. "I will see you tomorrow."

"I'll be there."

Was looked almost alarmed. "No, that's not what I meant. I'll stop by tomorrow after I get home."

Emily frowned. "But I thought—"

"And I appreciate the thought, but no."

"I'll sit in the back. Party manners." Her attempt at humor fell flat.

He held her face gently. "I don't want you there. If it's anything like my criminal trial, it will not be a high point in my life. So I'd rather not share it with someone who means so much to me."

She shook her head and met his stern look with defiance. "And because you mean something to me, I don't want you to go through that alone."

"I won't be. Delia will be there—like she was through the criminal trial."

She was relieved to hear Delia would be there, but she hated the thought of spending a day home not knowing how he was or what was happening to him. "So it's okay for Delia to see you like that but not me."

Wes clenched his jaw as his eyes bored through her with what looked like anger. "She's like family."

"And what about your family?"

"They don't know. My father's health isn't good, so he's too ill to travel. Since my parents can't be here, there's no point in worrying them."

She didn't like it, but it made sense. "Okay. But that's all the more reason for me to be there."

"Don't make this personal."

"Well, of course it's personal!" It was too late to hide her frustration.

"Come here." He opened his arms and drew her into an embrace, then he tenderly kissed her and cradled her head in his hands. "I know that you're trying to help, but please stay home tomorrow."

Emily didn't protest. But she didn't promise, either.

FOURTEEN

Wᴇs ᴡᴀʟᴋᴇᴅ from the bright morning sunlight into the courthouse. After passing through the scanners, he found his attorney, Kate Rychter, sitting on a bench in the hallway. With her, he was surprised to see, was his friend, criminal attorney Mike Chadwick.

Wes shook his hand. "Hi, Mike. Are you here to squeeze double billable hours out of me?"

Mike laughed. "I'm actually here as a friend—an unpaid one."

Their smiles faded, and Wes looked him in the eye. "Thanks, man."

Mike shrugged it off, but Wes knew he must have moved some things around in order to be there. He felt grateful to have such a friend.

Kate got right down to business. After explaining what to expect from the morning's proceedings, she lowered her voice. "Wes, I'm not going to lie. Your case doesn't look good. We tried to get some of the women to testify. For what it's worth, they were clearly conflicted. But they've got bills, and it would be hard on their families."

Wes nodded. "I never wanted to put them in that position—not in the criminal trial and not here."

She looked at him, her eyebrows furrowing. From the start, she had disagreed with his decision not to strongly encourage his former coworkers to testify, but he had been firm on that point.

Kate nodded. "I understand, but I think you know how much it weakens our position."

Wes's tone sharpened. "Kate, I get it. Don't worry about it. We've been through the worst in the criminal trial. What more can he do now except take my money?"

Mike quietly said, "Money's a nice thing to have."

Wes was in no mood to argue. Of course, what Mike was saying made perfect sense. "If the women I worked with were to testify now, yes, it might save me money but at their expense. It's just too high a price."

Kate and Mike exchanged looks but said nothing. Kate glanced at her watch. "Here we go." They got up and walked through the wood-paneled doors.

Wes tried to ignore the memories of his criminal trial, but while he could force most of those thoughts from his mind, his body was not so compliant. Twenty minutes had passed before his pulse slowed to almost normal and he stopped grinding his teeth. He could not understand why, in spite of all he'd been through, sitting here still took so much out of him. But Elliot must have hoped that he'd feel that way. Maybe Wes's discomfort was worth even more to Elliot than the money.

The opening statements went as Kate had predicted. And then Elliot Lewis took the stand. His version of events, false though it was, cast Wes in the worst possible light. By the end of his testimony, he'd laid out a convincing scenario of Wes as an office lothario who'd been possessive, if not downright obsessive, over Victoria for weeks.

Having been through this before, Wes could only sit numbly as the insults and lies were hurled at him. Kate cross-examined Lewis, but he was so used to lying that he was completely unruffled as he answered her questions. By the time Elliot Lewis stepped down from the stand, it was over. Wes knew it. From now on, it would be like watching a train wreck in slow motion. He knew how it would end, but it had to play out.

He glanced back at Delia. Emily sat beside her. He cast a sharp look her way then turned back toward the judge. He had specifically asked her not to come, and here she was, against his wishes. It did not help having her see him this way.

Kate gripped his hand. "Wes. You're on." After being sworn in, he told his version of the story. Then Elliot's attorney cross-examined.

"So let's back up to the point where you stood outside the door—a locked door—to your boss's office. Explain to the court why you broke down the door."

"I heard sounds of a struggle."

Lewis's lawyer lifted an eyebrow. "And how were you sure there was a struggle?"

"I heard Vic—Victoria."

"Was she talking?"

"No, more like grunting—"

"Or moaning?" The attorney lifted an eyebrow.

Wes glared at the lawyer and spoke slowly. "She didn't sound happy."

"You heard sounds, so you thought it was appropriate to break open the door."

"Yes. She was being assaulted."

"And how do you know that? Were there windows to see inside the office?"

"No." Anger roiled up within him, but he fought to stay calm.

"So in fact, you just guessed what was going on inside the office."

Wes eyed the attorney with suspicion. "Based on what I had observed in the past."

Lewis's attorney almost smiled with satisfaction. "Mr. Lewis has already testified, as you heard, that they were engaged in consensual sex. While not everyone would agree the office is the proper location for what they were doing, would you agree that consensual sex was their business and no one else's?"

"It became my business when I heard a woman struggling."

"And what led you to the conclusion that there was a struggle?"

"I heard her voice and other sounds."

The attorney's eyes lit as he lifted an eyebrow. "Did you hear a cry for help?"

"Her voice was muffled. I don't think she could speak."

"You don't think? But you don't know, do you?"

Wes glared at the attorney.

"Well, Mr. Taggert?"

"No."

"When the police arrived, who did they arrest?"

Wes saw where this was going. He clenched his jaw. "Me."

"So you broke into an office, destroyed company property, and brutally attacked your employer—an attack that resulted in his hospitalization—because you heard sounds."

Wes said nothing.

"And did the police arrest Mr. Lewis?"

"No."

"No. In fact, what happened to Mr. Lewis?"

"He was taken to the hospital—"

"Taken by whom?" the attorney asked.

"EMTs."

"Driving what?"

"An ambulance."

"I see. So you injured Mr. Lewis badly enough that an ambulance had to be called?"

"Yes."

"And when did they release him?"

Wes exhaled. "A week later."

"Mr. Lewis has testified that you repeatedly punched him in the face and banged his head against the floor."

"I was preventing a rape."

"And where was the woman at this time?"

"In the room."

"For the duration of the beating?"

Wes flashed a look at the attorney but then caught his own lawyer's eye. She had warned him that showing anger would hurt his case, so he tamped down his emotions. "I don't know. She was gone by the time... it was over."

"And did she go to the authorities and file a report?"

"I don't know. Not to my knowledge."

"Did she go to a doctor?" the attorney asked.

"I don't know."

"How well did you know Ms. Victoria Naylor?"

"We'd worked together on a couple of ad campaigns."

"How closely? Working lunches? Late nights at the office?"

Wes wanted to reach out and wipe that smirk off the face of Lewis's attorney, but a movement near the exit caught his attention. Emily was fleeing the courtroom, and Delia followed her out.

"Mr. Taggert, Did you have feelings for Ms. Victoria Naylor?"

"We were friends."

"Were you jealous of her relationship with Mr. Lewis?"

"She had no relationship—except as his employee." Wes took a deep breath. He refused to fall into the trap being laid for him. He would not lose his temper.

"You were just doing a good deed?" Lewis's attorney took a dramatic pause. "Well, that's quite a story."

Wes clenched his jaw as Lewis's lawyer proceeded to paint a picture of Wes as a jealous man who was so overcome with rage over losing his lover to his boss that he stormed in and attacked the poor man in a wild, uncontrollable rage. By the time he stepped down from the witness stand, Wes knew that he'd lost not only the case but Emily too. If only she had stayed home as he'd asked. But what good would it have done, really? If this hadn't happened, the publicity and people's reactions would have had the same effect. Whatever his relationship was with Emily, he was sure now that it was never meant to be. He was a fool to have hoped that it could work.

EMILY AND DELIA stood inside the main entrance of a lively brewpub—although any Boston beer hall was bound to be lively at that time of day. The place smelled of beer and fried foods, and the walls were lined with muted big screens displaying a number of games and commentators. A blond woman walked in and stood looking about.

"That's got to be her." Emily approached her. "Victoria?"

"Yes. You must be Emily."

Emily introduced Delia, and the three of them

walked past a sea of men and women in business-casual work garb, seated at long tables with backless benches on either side. In as quiet a corner as one could hope to find in a sports bar, Wes and his lawyers sat in a booth, engaged in intense conversation.

Delia and Victoria slipped into seats beside Wes, leaving Emily at the outside end of the horseshoe-shaped bench, too far for private conversation with Wes, which was how she preferred it right then. However, the distance did not stop him from directing a glare so intense that she thought molten mascara might flow down her cheeks at any minute.

After greetings and introductions, Emily got right to the point. "Victoria wants to testify."

Kate shared a look with Mike then turned to Victoria. "Why now? We asked you—more than once."

"Since the criminal trial. We've begged you!" added Mike.

"I know. I'm sorry. But I signed a nondisclosure agreement."

Kate did not mince words. "Yes, we know that. You told us that Lewis's lawyer made sure to include a hefty penalty if you violated it." Kate glanced at her watch. With twenty minutes before they were due back in court, she managed to simultaneously eat and look impatient. "So what's changed now?"

Vic glanced at Delia, who gave her an encouraging nod. "I've come into some money."

Kate set down her sandwich. "Today? In the middle of the trial? A large sum of money just fell into your lap?"

Mike leaned forward. "What Kate means is, you're not on the witness list. This isn't TV law, where surprise witnesses pop up like a jack-in-the-box at ten to the hour. In real life, that's not how it works." She and Mike shared a look, the nonverbal cues for which Emily translated to mean they were royally pissed.

Kate leveled her courtroom-examining look at Vic. "Who gave you the money?"

Vic looked down.

Kate glanced at Wes, then her voice took on a no-nonsense tone. "Tell me now. Because if it comes out in court that Wes is paying you off, it'll just hurt his case."

Victoria fidgeted with a cocktail napkin. "It was a gift from someone who knew what I'd been through."

"I did it." Delia lifted her chin.

Stunned silence followed.

"Well, don't look so shocked. I'm no Warren Buffet, but I've got a few dollars I haven't spent yet."

Wes turned to her, but before he could speak, Delia put her hand on his. "I'm pretty sure I never paid you for that last lawn-mowing job, so I owed you. That compounded interest is a bitch."

Kate shook her head. "The judge will demand to know where it came from."

Delia's expression went blank, but she quickly recovered. "We have a nondisclosure agreement." She pulled a pen from her purse, scribbled something on a napkin, and slid it to Victoria. "Sign this, please." After Victoria signed the napkin, Delia handed it to Kate. "For your files."

Kate leveled a stare at Delia, then she turned to Wes. "Can we clone her?"

Wes said, "You'd have to, 'cause she's one of a kind."

Kate looked at Mike, who lifted his eyebrows. "So our case strategy has come down to a Hail Mary pass?"

Mike nodded. "It might be Wes's best chance."

Kate shook her head. "Let's hope the judge is in a generous mood."

Mike turned to Vic. "We could've used you during the criminal trial."

Kate chimed in. "Not to mention at the beginning of the civil trial—when we asked you."

Wes cut them off. "It was my fault. I told her not to. Even if she'd had the money to pay off Lewis, she would have dragged her name—and her kids' and her parents'—through the mud. I told her no, and I'll live with the consequences."

"I'm afraid you will have to." Kate glanced at Mike.

"You know what the judge will think—that we paid her to testify. The timing couldn't be worse. Oh well." She took a breath and then turned to Vic. "Tell me everything that happened that day."

Five minutes later, Mike interrupted. "It's time."

Wes settled the lunch bill, and they rushed out of the pub. Kate was still pumping Victoria for information as they walked back to court.

Emily was grateful to Delia for positioning herself between her and Wes as a buffer. The last thing Wes needed was to appear distraught in court.

As soon as court was back in session, Kate asked to approach the bench. The two attorneys stood before the judge, speaking in quiet but heated tones. When the judge shook his head and the lawyers turned around, it was clear that he would not allow Victoria to testify. Wes had lost his last chance. From that point on, although Wes's lawyers gave it their best effort, at the end of the day, the judge wasted no time in ruling for the plaintiff. It was over. Wes had lost.

As they all walked together out to the parking lot, Mike told Wes, "Hey, man, I'm sorry. We tried."

Wes nodded abstractedly.

Emily whispered to Delia. "The attorney's fees are

even more than the damages. Does he have it? Will he be okay?"

Delia said, "I honestly don't know how much is in his trust. I've gotten the impression that he could manage the trial. But whether he'll have anything left to live on, I don't know."

They thanked Vic again for trying. She was clearly upset. "I wish I hadn't listened to you. If I'd come forward before..."

Wes lifted her hands and held them in his. "You did all that you could, and I thank you."

Her face wrinkled as tears filled her eyes. "You did everything for me, and I'll never forget it." She gave him a hug and got into her car.

When the rest had all said their goodbyes, Emily went to the passenger door of Delia's car, but Wes grasped her elbow before she could get in. He looked over the top of the car. "Delia, would you mind if Emily rode back with me?"

Without taking her eyes from him, Delia said, "I think you're asking the wrong person." Her gaze shifted to Emily.

Emily glanced upward at Wes and then down. She exhaled and gave Delia a knowing look. "Thanks for everything. I'll talk to you soon." She turned and walked with Wes to his car. "Just don't yell at me while you're driving. That's all I ask."

FIFTEEN

THEY WERE HALFWAY HOME, and Wes hadn't uttered a word. Emily turned from the window she'd been staring through for the past hour and a half. "Is this why you asked me to ride with you—so you could give me the silent treatment?"

Wes pulled off the highway and filled up the tank, then he drove down a back road and into a parking lot at the recreation area under the Sagamore Bridge. There he stopped the car and got out then walked around to open Emily's door. He took her hand, and they went to the water and looked out at the boats passing by in the Cape Cod Canal.

"I thought it wouldn't feel so bad this time around, since it couldn't be worse than the last time. I mean, there was no fear of prison. But it does something to your soul to be wrongly accused. I think I'll just carry that with me the rest of my life." He turned to her. "I didn't want you to see me like that."

"Like what—being human?" She looked at him with sympathy.

He looked down, and his mouth turned up slightly at the corners. "It's a little early in the relationship for that, don't you think?"

Emily tilted her head. "Well, I guess. But I only date humans, so..." She shrugged. "But good job trying to shake me off."

"I can't get rid of you, can I?" He turned and focused those brilliant-blue eyes on her, a sight that never failed to make her heart beat faster.

She grinned. "No, not yet. But who knows? In time, if you're lucky..."

He drew her against him and wrapped his arms about her. "I hope I'm never that lucky." He kissed her softly as the boats drifted down the canal.

THE FOLLOWING AFTERNOON, Delia knocked on Emily's door. "Would you grab one of these bags?" Emily took one of Delia's cloth shopping bags. "It's a six-pack of beer. There's another one in this bag. We're going to Wes's. The pizza should be there in the next ten minutes."

Emily smoothed her hair into place. "Does he know that we're coming?"

"Not exactly. Can I use your phone? I'll give him a five-minute warning."

"Good. That gives me time to maybe comb my hair and put on some lipstick."

As Delia dialed Wes's number, she said, "That's the great thing about growing old. No one cares whether or not you're wearing lipstick. Now, not wearing pants might be more of a problem, but for the most part, expectations get lower." She turned toward the window and spoke into the phone. "Wes? Delia. I'm on my way over. Oh, here comes the pizza delivery. It's on me. I've paid him and tipped him already, so just take the box. We'll be there in a minute or two."

If Wes protested, Emily couldn't tell from the smile on Delia's face. "Come on. We've got some cheering up to do."

Five minutes later, the three of them were sitting at the table on Wes's deck, drinking beer, eating pizza, and discussing finances.

"Look, I appreciate what you've done, what you're doing—all of it—but it's over." He let out a deep, weary sigh. "Finally over."

Delia leaned forward, elbows on the table. "I just want to make sure you're okay money-wise."

He lifted his eyes and looked at Delia. "If you're

asking whether things are dire—no, they're not. Austere maybe."

Emily started to get up. "I'll go get... uh... some napkins." Then she spied a huge pile on the table.

Wes put his hand on her wrist. "Sit down. It's okay. You already know the worst about me."

"I don't want to pry."

"That might've been something to think about yesterday during the trial. But this? I don't care."

His words stung. "I'm sorry."

He touched her hand. "No, I'm sorry. I seem to be a little short-tempered these days."

His soft look melted her heart. "All I've ever wanted to do was to help."

"I know. If it hadn't been for you and Delia, I'd be in even worse shape than I already am." He looked at Delia. "I've gone through nearly all of the trust. I live pretty simply. I don't need a lot. But if I run out, I can always mow lawns." He smiled.

Delia got another slice of pizza. "Your rent's free, of course—until better days come."

He laughed. "Have you looked at my days lately? They don't seem to be trending that way." His expression grew somber. "Thanks, but I'll pay my own rent. You've done more than enough."

"I only wish I could have helped more. The good news is, since Vic didn't have to testify, she didn't have to pay Lewis for breaking their agreement. That left-over money should cover your rent for a couple of years. So that's settled." Delia stood. "Oh, look. I'm out of beer. I'll go get us another round." She was gone before he could protest.

Wes reached over and entwined his fingers in Emily's. "I guess about now you're wishing there'd been a vacant cottage on down the road or across town —anywhere but here."

Emily looked into his eyes. "Stop. I won't listen to any more talk like that."

"Talk like what?"

"Like your value as a man is measured by your bank balance."

He rolled his eyes. "I don't mean it that way—not exactly. I mean, I'd be okay—I was okay on my own. But if I'm going to involve other people in my life..." He gave her a knowing look. "It's not easy being with me. There are issues I'll need to work through. I'm just saying it's going to be a long time before I'm back on my feet."

"I know. Tell me about it." She stretched out her leg and lifted her orthopedic boot. "I guess we'll have to be off our feet together." She gave him a mischievous look just as Delia returned.

Delia placed a fresh beer in each of their hands. "So, what did I miss?"

Emily grinned. "The short version is, Wes will be fine, thanks to people like you."

Delia looked out at the sea. "Someone once said that living well is the best revenge. But I don't think that only means money. I can't imagine how someone like Lewis could ever truly be happy. People like that spend their whole lives chasing something that they'll never catch. Their own insolvent souls elude them, but they're too blinded by self-deception to figure that out."

SIXTEEN

Em,

I'm going away for a while. I need some time to sort through some things. I thought life would go on—and it will, just not now. Sorry, Em. There's no mystery here. I'm just not ready—for anything, really.

—Wes

Emily knew the letter by heart. She'd read it many times since she'd found it slid under her door. She handed it to her landlady as the two of them sat at Delia's kitchen table.

"He just slipped it under the door. I should have seen it coming. We got too close, and he bolted."

Delia stared out the window. "He's been through a lot. But I wouldn't write him off yet."

Emily frowned and waved her hand toward the note. "I'm not the one doing the writing."

"He'll come back."

"Oh, I don't doubt he'll come home—just not to me." She blinked away tears that threatened to spill.

Delia said nothing. After trying so hard to match up Wes and Emily, she had figured out when to stay silent.

Emily stared at her coffee mug. "I shouldn't let my feelings get carried away. I came here to escape all that. This was supposed to be all about me, about pulling my life back together. And now look at me. It's all about Wes, and my life's falling apart."

Delia smiled gently. "Are our lives ever really together? Maybe it's all about you moving on with your life."

"But I wanted to move on with Wes."

Delia got up, brought over the coffeepot, and refilled Emily's coffee. "I've known Wes since he was a boy. He doesn't take anything lightly, so whatever he's told you, he meant it."

Emily smirked. "I'm not sure how helpful that is."

Delia shrugged. "Take that note, for instance. Why did he leave it for you?"

"So I'd know."

"Because...?"

"Okay. Because there's something between us—but it's nebulous at best—and now probably over."

"Could be, but I doubt it. Right now, he's got too many emotions at war in his head and his heart. I don't pretend to understand men, but I know Wes well enough to know that you mean something to him. Try to see it from his point of view. He's been through a traumatic ordeal that has... well, I don't want to say *ruined*, but it has turned his life upside down."

"I know, but..."

"On top of that, he's already overwhelmed with emotion, and then you come along. Maybe he just needs time to catch his breath and feel back in control of his life."

"Oh, great. So he's off getting control of his life at the expense of mine." Emily leaned back and sighed.

Delia set down her coffee. "And maybe he's gone away because he cares so much for you that he wants to do what's best for you."

Emily couldn't contain her frustration. "Well, that's just stupid. He's what's best for me."

Delia smiled. "He just needs to figure that out. Give him time. Patience wouldn't be considered a virtue if it came easily."

Emily grumbled. "I don't want to be virtuous. I want to be with him."

Delia gave Emily a sympathetic smile and took a sip of her coffee.

Wᴇꜱ ꜱᴀᴛ at a picnic table next to a roadside crab shack. A fresh lobster roll and a bowl of clam chowder were all he needed or wanted from life anymore. Except for Emily. While downing a lobster roll in record time, he watched people waiting in line. Everyone ate at that shack sooner or later if they knew what was good for them. They came from all walks of life. Good food was good food. As he looked at them all standing there, he couldn't have said whose life was happier. Some had gotten out of expensive cars while others pulled up in old beaters. Simple pleasures shared with good friends meant more than the nightclubs and parties he'd attended while living the dream at the ad agency. The idea was nothing new. He'd always felt that way. But now there was one thing—or one person—who had changed everything.

His feelings for Emily had taken him by surprise. Maybe that was what scared him the most. He felt as if he'd had no choice in the matter. He'd met her, he'd gotten to know her, and the next thing he knew, he was watching her fall on her way to the lighthouse. And he was off, running as fast as he could, because he had to help her. It didn't matter that her fiancé was next door. Wes was running to Emily because he cared about her more than anyone else possibly could. There was a name for that feeling, but he wasn't ready to think it let alone say it. The power of it terrified him.

He finished his chowder and headed back to his tent. He'd gotten permission to pitch it on the dunes in front of a friend's beachfront home. The owner had offered Wes full use of the house, since he wouldn't be there for the next couple of weeks. But Wes had declined.

All he wanted was a tent, a cooler of beer, and the sound of the ocean to settle his mind. He wasn't sure how long that would take. His mind was hopelessly unsettled. But he'd stay there until he could figure it out. Was that too much to ask?

WES LOOKED at his beard in his driver's-side mirror. It was a beard to be proud of, a week's worth of growth. Of course, he also had a week's worth of smell to go with it. As he looked at the sun peeking over the horizon, he took a deep breath then exhaled. He'd been overthinking this process called living. In truth, it was a simple matter of eating, sleeping, and coexisting with one's surroundings. But if, in the midst of it all, one found someone to share it with, that was worth more than a career, misplaced pride or, most of all, money. All he truly needed in life was at home, or close to it in

Emily's cottage. And he would go to her and tell her —that day.

He packed up his tent and gear and drove home. But when he pulled into the driveway, Emily's car was gone. He'd been away for a week. Had she given up on him so easily? He pulled out his phone. "Delia, where is she?"

After a second of silence, she said, "I gather you mean Emily?"

He didn't even try to conceal his frustration. "Well, yes! Who else would I mean? Do you know where she is?"

"I'm sorry, but I haven't a clue. I'm only the landlord."

He couldn't decide whether the edge in her voice came from annoyance or amusement. He knew one thing: he felt like a jerk for the tone he had taken. "I'm sorry. I didn't mean to—"

"Snap? It's all right. Just remember I'm on your side. Okay?"

"Yeah. I'm really sorry."

"It's okay," Delia said.

After at least two more apologies, Wes hung up the phone and unpacked his camping gear. As he closed his garage door, a car pulled into the driveway next door. He bounded inside to get a better view from his bathroom window, which faced Emily's house. She was home.

He clenched both fists in a victory gesture then turned and caught sight of himself in the mirror. "Oh, yeah. Guess I'd better shave, or she won't recognize me." He lifted his arm and took a whiff. "Whew! And shower."

SEVENTEEN

FIFTEEN MINUTES LATER, he knocked on her door. When it opened, he said, "I thought we might go out to dinner."

The door closed in his face. "And I love you," he said to the door. Her window was open. He leaned over and called inside. "Emily? Emily! Please, can we talk?"

The door opened. "You've been gone for a week."

"Yeah." The guilt was almost too much to bear.

"Yeah." She stared at him—or through him. He couldn't be sure.

This was not how he'd planned it. He looked up to the heavens. *If the great master plan for my life was for me to be humbled, mission accomplished.* "So I thought we might talk."

Her face went from anger to disbelief—and indignation. "Yeah, I thought we might talk too—before you took off for your fortress of solitude with no warning and no explanation."

"I'm... sorry." Feeling defeated, he turned and headed for home. *Well, that went well.*

"Wes!"

He was done. He'd bared his soul. She had stomped on it—well, maybe not *stomped*, but she'd left a well-defined footprint. He couldn't take any more. But the manners he'd been raised with forced him to stop when she called out to him. He turned and met her unwavering gaze.

She tilted her head toward the doorway. "Come in."

As he walked inside, she waved a hand toward the sofa. She sat down in a chair. *Because it would be crazy to hope she'd sit next to me on the same piece of furniture.*

She wasted no time. "First of all, you leave me a cryptic note saying you're going away for a while. Did that mean for a week—for a month? Then you show up on my doorstep with no warning—like you assume I'm just waiting for you and my feelings don't matter. You've met Oliver. Been there, done that."

He winced. Did she have to compare him to Oliver? There might have been worse things she could have said, but this ranked pretty far up there. He took a breath. "You're right. I should've manned up and talked with you first."

"Yes, you should have." She was not going to let him off easily.

"But I knew that my feelings would get in the way and I'd cave." He could see from her expression that his words had come out all wrong.

"*Cave*, meaning stay with me?"

She looked like she might stand up and show him the door, so he had to get right to the point. "*Cave*, meaning I love you so much I can't think clearly around you." He glanced at her eyes and thanked God that what he saw wasn't hate or even annoyance. He felt safe to keep going. "I wanted everything to be perfect for you. When I couldn't make it perfect, I doubted myself and wondered whether I was just being selfish. And then there's the pressure. I'm in no way prepared to support you."

She leaned away from him and looked about. "I'm sorry, have we just time traveled? 'Cause I left my apron and pumps back in 1955."

Wes frowned as he stammered. "I mean, not that I'm—that we're—but, you know, eventually..."

"Keep going." Her mouth quirked.

"No."

Was she laughing at him? Maybe it was just an

affectionate smile. No, it was laughter. *You can't hear a smile.*

She held up her palm. "Wes, what are you talking about?"

"Us."

"Well, I'm glad there's an *us*, because after you left, I thought maybe I'd lost us, and I missed it. I missed you."

"Em, I missed you. But I needed to figure it out."

She nodded. "So now that you've figured it out, would you mind telling me what 'it' is?"

"My life. And I want you in it."

Her eyes softened, but she'd been so unpredictable that he didn't dare follow his instincts, which told him to go to her, put his mouth on hers, and kiss her until next week.

"And one more thing," he said.

She said softly, "What?"

"I love you."

He thought she might cry, but the next moment, her face wrinkled to a petulant frown. "Well, you could have said that sooner."

"I did. But you closed the door, so you might not have heard me."

She exhaled. "Maybe I love you too."

He stood and took hold of her hands and pulled her to her feet. "Just maybe?"

"I'll let you know in a week or two—after I figure it out," she said, though by the expression in her eyes, she had already figured it out. "In the meanwhile, would you kiss me? It might help me decide."

He didn't have to be told twice. He kissed her and held her against him and kissed her again.

She whispered, "Say it again."

Wes shook his head. "Oh no. That's not how it works. I said it, and now you have to say it."

"I did!"

"Maybes don't count."

"Says who?"

"Says my mouth, which is not going to kiss you until you admit it. You love me."

Her lips spread into a smile. "I do."

"Still doesn't count till you say all three words."

"I love you, for crying out loud."

"Too many. Just three."

She feigned confusion. "Crying. Out. Loud?"

"Come here." He pulled her into his arms. His lips brushed hers. "You are so very close."

"Wes Taggert, I love you."

He considered for a second. "That's five, but I'll take it." He kissed her, and she said it again. "I like the sound of that."

A WEEK PASSED, and the newness of love settled comfortably upon them. They stood on the dunes. From the distant horizon, the setting sun set the seawater ablaze in a bright amber glow. Together, they picked out a spot on the beach. Wes started building a fire, while Emily set down her bags and unfolded the chairs.

She reached into one of the bags, pulled out a bottle of wine, and uncorked it. "This Australian Merlot is a perfect pairing with those hot dogs."

Wes turned around long enough to smirk. "You know it's the good stuff when it comes in an extra-large bottle."

"Well, yeah. Like I didn't know that already." She grinned and proceeded to pour wine into two clear plastic cups, one of which she held out to him. "This will fuel you while you fuel that fire."

Wes happily took it and watched as the kindling caught fire. He got up from his crouched position and settled into a chair beside Emily. Taking hold of her hand, he looked out toward the water as the seagulls called out, swooped down to the water, and soared back up to the sky.

"Life doesn't get any better than this—a cool sea breeze, a warm fire, and dinner out." He took a sip of wine and leaned his head back on the chair.

Emily sighed. "It's perfect."

His forehead creased. "I don't understand you."

"What's not to understand? I'm just a simple girl."

He chuckled. "Oh, I doubt that. But you're kind."

She wrinkled her face. "I try to be, but what are you talking about?"

Wes smiled to himself. "Never mind. I'm just feeling lucky that you're here with me."

Emily feigned annoyance. "Now, don't start that again."

"Start what?"

"You know." She knew how much it bothered him to have his life up in the air. And she knew that, in a convoluted sort of way, she'd made it worse. He had a hard time letting go of the idea that he should bring something to the relationship, like financial stability, gainful employment, or some sort of hunter-gatherer getup. She wasn't bothered by any of it. He wasn't lazy or lacking ambition. To the contrary, he seemed to feel useless without something to strive for. Whether by nature or nurture, the need for goals was hardwired into his thinking, which wasn't a bad thing in itself. It was good to set standards and goals for one's life under ordinary circumstances, but these were not.

Still leaning back in her chair, Emily turned her head toward him. "Give yourself permission to relax for a while. After what you've been through, you deserve it."

She couldn't quite read the facial expression that followed. It held a mixture of guilt, gratitude, and maybe love.

Their cell phones both dinged at the same time. Emily reached into the bag that was closest to her and pulled out her phone. The cell signals were spotty out on the dunes, but texts sometimes came through.

Wes was already reading his screen. "Delia just got out of a meeting of her lighthouse committee. They submitted our campaign for an award for nonprofits."

Emily stared at her screen with wide eyes. "Oh. Well, I guess it's a good way to draw more attention to the cause."

He peered at her with a crooked smile. "And to us —since we won!"

"What?" Emily went through a few degrees of disbelief then lifted her eyebrows in wonder. "We won an award."

"I think I just said that."

"I know. I just can't believe it."

"Believe it. And not only that, but our lighthouse campaign is killing it—not just with the award but the online donations as well. We're sixty thousand dollars away from our goal!"

Emily was beaming as she lifted her clear-plastic wine cup in a toast. "Well, hot damn! Here's to us. What a team!"

Wes touched his glass to hers. "Let's celebrate with some fire-roasted hot dogs."

"Excellent choice, sir. And maybe a refill on that wine?"

"By all means!"

EMILY PULLED two mugs from her cabinet and filled them with coffee. "Well, it had to rain sometime, I guess." She handed one mug to Wes and sat down at her kitchen table.

"I don't mind, really. I get more work done on rainy days. Or did—when I had work to do." He took a sip and stared at the rain drizzling down the window.

Emily watched Wes. Then, deep in thought, her gaze drifted down to the table. For a few silent minutes, she considered whether to bring up the topic. "Funny thing—I've been thinking about something since we finished the lighthouse campaign."

Wes made a sharp turn from the window. "It's a nice idea, but it just wouldn't work."

"You don't even know what it is yet."

He lowered his chin and looked deeply into her eyes. "Let me guess. It has something to do with us working together."

Emily slowly leaned back in her chair. "Was I really so horrible to work with?"

Wes heaved a sigh. "No. You're fantastically talented and incredibly easy to work with."

"Well, that explains it, then." He was making polite excuses. What else could it be?

"I've thought about it. But it costs money to start up a business."

Emily shrugged. "I've got some of that set aside. I'm not saying it's enough to live large and rent an office building, but we could start on a small scale and work from home."

Halfway through her sentence, he began shaking his head. "If I can't bring anything to the table, I won't come to the table at all."

"Well, you just came to my table and took that coffee I handed to you."

Wes rolled his eyes. "And I was happy to do it. But there's a limit to how much hospitality I'll accept. A dollar's worth of coffee is one thing. Accepting thousands of dollars for business expenses is something quite different."

Emily was not willing to give up so easily. "The lighthouse campaign didn't cost us a thing."

"Because they had the cash ready to finance our work. What happens when we're three months into a campaign and not getting paid? We need to have something to carry us over in case cash-flow situations arise —and they will."

Emily could practically hear the hiss of her spirits deflating. "If it would make you feel better, we can call it a loan. Maybe your lawyer friend Mike would draw up a promissory note for us. In fact, there are probably forms on the Internet." She leaned closer. "But that would just be for you, 'cause I trust you."

"You shouldn't trust anyone where money is concerned."

"You're just throwing out platitudes as a smoke-screen to avoid the real issue. I get it. You don't want to go into business together, so we won't." She stood, took her cup and spoon to the sink, and washed them vigorously.

Wes followed and stood behind her, circling her waist with his arms. As he nuzzled his face in her neck, he said, "I love the idea. Let's just give it some time so we can figure this out."

Emily set down the dish she was washing. "The last time you needed to figure something out, you disappeared for a week."

"And where was the first place I went when I came back?" He pivoted her around and gave her a look with those gorgeous blue eyes.

"Well, that's just not fair. I just got my walking

boot off, and here you go, making me weak in the knees."

A satisfied twinkle came to his eyes. "Welcome to my world." He gave her a kiss that nearly made her forget what they'd been talking about. "I promise I'll do all my thinking within a one-mile radius of my home. Since that includes yours, will that meet with your satisfaction?"

She had to say, "Yes, I guess so." But she couldn't resist adding, "But just remember that working together could solve so many problems."

"How many?"

She grimaced. "I haven't counted. Maybe you can do that while you're thinking."

He smiled as though he found frustration charming. Then he pulled her closer and did an even better job of driving all thoughts of business away.

EIGHTEEN

A SUMMER SHOWER dampened their original plan to go sailing, so Wes and Emily went for a drive. They picked up some takeout seafood and went to the Cape Cod National Seashore, where they sat in a picnic pavilion surrounded by the sounds of the rain on the roof and on the rustling leaves. There they ate and talked about everything except going into business together.

Since they'd known one another, their lives—especially Wes's—had been steeped in such turmoil that they agreed that taking things slowly would be the best way to proceed. Emily had just broken off her engagement, and Wes had just lost not only a civil lawsuit but also most of the funds in the trust his grandparents had left him. Admitting he'd fallen in love had been, Emily realized, a huge step on his part. So if taking things slowly helped Wes, she wouldn't deny him the time that he needed.

The late-afternoon sun cast an orange path over the water as Wes pulled into his driveway. "Your place or mine?"

Emily smiled and, without hesitation, said, "Mine."

"Should I take that personally?"

"No, not at all. I love the whole bachelor-pad ambience, but I'm in the mood for something..."

"Cleaner?" A guilty smile followed.

"I was going to say *different*, but okay, cleaner." She laughed.

As soon as they walked into her cottage, Wes took Emily into his arms. "You sit down and relax, and I'll take care of our beverage needs."

"Thank you!" She sank into the sofa and turned on the TV.

As Wes returned with two bottles of beer, Emily leaned forward. "Wes! Look!"

A Boston newscaster stood, microphone in hand. "I'm here outside the Superior Court building, where prominent Boston businessman Elliot Lewis has been arraigned for the alleged sexual assault of a female employee. He has entered a plea of not guilty. However, we have just confirmed that, since his arrest, three more women have come forward with similar charges."

Wes pulled out his phone.

"Wes?"

He held his phone up to Emily and showed her a text message from Vic that read, "I did it."

He and Vic texted back and forth for a minute or two while Emily tried to decide whether to cry or cheer —or both. Then Wes put his phone down and turned a stunned face to Emily. "The civil trial upset her. She finally had the funds—thanks to Delia—to break the nondisclosure agreement. So when her testimony was barred, she couldn't let it go. And although she didn't come out and say it, she knew what it would do to her family. It took a few days, but she made an appointment with Kate, who called Mike into the meeting. All I can say is, everyone needs a college buddy who went on to law school... Mike canceled his afternoon plans and went straight to the police station with her."

Emily had no words. She could only throw her arms about Wes.

By the time the initial shock subsided, Vic had sent Wes two more texts. Still shaking his head in disbelief, he turned to Emily. "They're planning to give Elliot Lewis a taste of his own medicine—first a criminal trial, then a civil proceeding. A number of his employees have agreed to come forward, so it sounds like they'll be able to bury him in evidence of his guilt. If all goes as planned, Elliot Lewis can look forward to a long stay at the steel-bar hotel."

EMILY SAT ON HER PORCH, sipping coffee, still stunned by the news of the previous day. She looked next door. Wes was on his deck, pacing and talking.

Minutes later, he came over and joined her. "I just got an interesting call." He looked barely able to contain his delight, so it had to be good news.

"Oh?"

He smiled, eyes shining. "Yes, Vic and a handful of others are forming an ad firm."

"Well, that's great. So there's life after the Lewis Ad Agency." She could tell from his face that there was more. She did her best to be patient, but he was taking great pleasure in drawing it out.

"And they've asked me to join them."

"Well, that's great!" It didn't feel all that great from her point of view, but it was a great opportunity for him. "So? Of course you said yes."

"No, I didn't."

Emily exhaled and grimaced. "Don't tell me it's the

money again. This is a great opportunity. You could apply for a business loan. You'll be a hero by the end of the trial. No one would turn you down now."

His eyes softened. "I told her no because I've got another job lined up."

She didn't expect that. Maybe she needed a week at her own fortress of solitude. "Oh, really?"

"Working with you." He gave her a toothy white grin of amusement.

"I hope you enjoyed that, because I didn't." She pretended to scowl, but she was so thoroughly happy that she couldn't maintain the facade.

"I did, thank you. When Vic started talking about business loans, it occurred to me that now I could get one of my own for my share of our business."

"Gosh, why didn't we think of that sooner?" It was Emily's turn to grin as Wes pulled her out of her chair and into his arms. "So this is happening—Taggert and Cooke."

She scrunched up her face.

"What?" he asked.

"I don't know. It just doesn't have the right ring to it."

Wes looked at her, puzzled.

Her face brightened. "I've got it!"

He lifted his eyebrows, waiting.

"Cooke and Taggert!" She nodded. "So much better, don't you think?"

With a knowing smile, he said, "I think it sounds great. Come here, Cooke."

"Okay, Taggert." Emily threw her arms around his neck and sealed the deal with a kiss.

NINETEEN

One Year Later

WES OPENED the car door for Emily, who emerged in a simple and elegant black dress.

"You look gorgeous."

She smiled. "It's new. I retired my all-purpose little black dress when I quit my job at the college." She took a moment to take in Wes's appearance.

He smoothed back his hair and looked down at his chest and his arms. "You're staring. What's the matter? Do I have something hanging out of my nose?"

Emily laughed. "I'm staring because you don't look half bad in a tux."

He wrinkled his face. "Don't get too used to it. As soon as this is over, the tux goes straight to the back of my closet."

"Well, that's just a shame." She ran her fingertips over his shirt buttons. "Because you look so good that who knows, you might just get lucky."

"Yeah? Excuse me while I go call my tailor and order ten more." He slipped his arm around her waist and led her toward the lighthouse.

As they neared the building with its fresh white paint and new windows, a dozen people scurried about, setting up chairs and tables. Lights were already strung up, and several posters on easels displayed Emily's graphic along with photos showing the work at various stages of progress. The day had arrived. After all the hard work of so many people, they would now dedicate the refurbished lighthouse.

Emily turned to Wes. "I don't see anyone here but the catering staff. Is there some reason you wanted to get here so early?"

"Punctuality is a virtue."

Emily frowned. "I thought that was patience."

"Yeah, that too." He took hold of her hand and led her to the lighthouse door, which he held open for her. "Come on. While we're waiting for everyone else, let's go up to the lantern room and look at the view."

As they rounded the last of the stairs, Emily gripped the rail. "Slight fear of heights."

He turned around, looking worried. "Should we go back down?"

"No, I'm okay. I just needed a minute. I'm fine now."

Wes took hold of her hand. "I won't let go. I promise. Wanted to show you this three-hundred-sixty-degree view. It's spectacular."

"Look, you can see our two cottages."

"Such a waste." He shook his head as he stared at their homes.

"What's such a waste?"

"Paying for rent on two cottages."

She eyed him with suspicion. "Well, at the rate our business is going, it won't be long before we can afford two large beach homes."

"What if we settled for one?"

Before she could think of how to answer, Wes dropped to one knee. He looked up at her with a mixture of adoration and trepidation. "I brought you here because this lighthouse brought us together, and I'm hoping it will bring us a new life together."

Too stunned to move and almost too stunned to breathe, Emily watched as he pulled a ring from his pocket.

"Will you marry me, Emily Cooke?"

It was all she could do to get the word out past the sudden flood of emotions. "Yes."

From that moment, everything was a blur—mainly because of the tears in her eyes. Wes took her left hand

and slipped a cushion-cut sapphire ring onto it. Then he stood and kissed her and held her. He exhaled deeply.

"What's wrong?"

"I'm just so relieved you said yes."

She looked at him as though he'd lost his mind. "And what did you think I was going to say?"

"I don't know. No? Or that you needed some time to think?"

"You're the one who takes time."

"That's what I was afraid of—that you'd seize this moment to exact your revenge for my taking off for a week to go camping."

She slowly nodded. "You know, that's not such a bad idea."

He interrupted her with a kiss, followed by a warm smile. "Say what you will, but I think this was one of my better decisions."

Emily's heart swelled with emotion. "I may not agree with your process, but I do like the outcome."

Wes slipped his fingers through the hair at the nape of her neck and kissed her, then they stood arm in arm and looked out at the view from the top of the lighthouse, which at that moment felt like the top of the world.

AFTER DREAMING and planning their future together, the newly engaged couple emerged from the lighthouse. With ten minutes to go before the ceremony began, most of the guests had arrived. The warm summer night was filled with the gentle murmur and the punctuation of laughter as people made their way to their seats.

"You two look very happy."

Emily and Wes both turned, sporting ear-to-ear grins. Delia had appeared out of nowhere, and they'd been too preoccupied to notice.

"We are," they said. They had decided to wait until after the ceremony to share their good news.

Delia looked up at the lighthouse and the beacon of light it sent out to sea. "It's a good feeling to arrive at the end of a journey like this. It's been quite a year."

"Yes, it has." Emily felt that her eyes had to be nearly as bright as the lighthouse.

Just in time, Delia excused herself and went up to the podium. This had been her brainchild, and now she would lead the celebration to its completion.

The ceremony ended, and Delia was much in demand during the champagne reception as people offered their thanks and congratulations. But in time, the crowd thinned, and the last of the catering staff packed up and left, leaving the three of them on a bench with a bottle of champagne.

Wes filled Delia's glass and lifted his own in a toast. "You, Delia Langdon, have accomplished a wonderful thing."

Delia's eyes twinkled. "So have you, it seems."

Before Wes could express his confusion in words, Delia pointed to Emily's ring. "I don't know which gives off more light—the lighthouse or that ring. So when did this happen?" Delia reached out and gestured for Emily to hold out her hand and give her a closer look at the ring.

"Just before you arrived." Emily waited while Delia admired her ring.

Wes put his arm around Emily's shoulder. "We wanted to tell you before, but we didn't want to distract you before the dedication."

Delia squeezed Emily's hand and released it. "So I have two accomplishments to celebrate tonight. Bringing you two together was clearly the more challenging one."

Wes slipped his arm from Emily's shoulder and clasped her hand. "This is clearly my favorite, but I still marvel at how you pulled it all off—especially that last fifty-thousand-dollar donation for the lighthouse. I can't help but wonder who that anonymous donor could be."

Delia shrugged and smiled.

"Now, wait a minute." Emily narrowed her eyes. "I'm not buying it. You know who it is."

Delia feigned innocence.

Emily shook her head. "I've put some thought into this mystery. It had to be somebody who really cared about this particular lighthouse. Probably somebody local who adores the lighthouse and what it means to this community." As Emily spoke, Wes leveled a knowing look at Delia. "Sound familiar?"

Delia's eyes softened. "I imagine it's someone who prefers to live simply and spend money in careful but important ways."

Wes lifted his glass in a toast. "Here's to people like that."

The three toasted and leaned back in the bench that looked out to sea, where the reflection from the Hope Harbor Lighthouse lit a path to their dreams of the future.

ACKNOWLEDGMENTS

Editing by Red Adept Editing
redadeptediting.com

THANK YOU!

Thank you, reader. With so many options, I appreciate your choosing my book to read. Your opinion matters, so please consider sharing a review to help other readers.

BOOK NEWS

Would you like to know when the next book comes out? Click below to sign up for the J.L. Jarvis Journal and get book news, free books, and exclusive content delivered monthly.

news.jljarvis.com

ABOUT THE AUTHOR

J.L. Jarvis is a left-handed opera singer/teacher/lawyer who writes books. She received her undergraduate training from the University of Illinois at Urbana-Champaign and a doctorate from the University of Houston. She now lives and writes in upstate New York.

Sign up to be notified of book releases and related news:
news.jljarvis.com

Email JL at:
writer@jljarvis.com

Follow JL online at:
jljarvis.com

facebook.com/jljarvis1writer

twitter.com/JLJarvis_writer

instagram.com/jljarvis.writer

bookbub.com/authors/j-l-jarvis

pinterest.com/jljarviswriter

goodreads.com/5106618.J_L_Jarvis

amazon.com/author/B005G0M2Z0

youtube.com/UC7kodjlaG-VcSZWhuYUUl_Q

Made in the USA
Monee, IL
17 May 2021